Sugar Spinelli's Little Instruction Book

Why, would you look at that? Jessica Fremont is here—and she's got a bidding number! Her mama-in-law isn't going to like this at all. A bachelor auction—even for charity—is just too much fun for the high-and-mighty Fremonts. But Jessica only married into the Fremonts, and from what I remember, she was pretty wild in her salad days. Gave Rachel Fremont fits when her son all but eloped with the gal. Jessica settled down, though, and from all accounts has fit into the Fremont mold. It was a shame that her husband died so soon after they were married, leaving her with a baby and all. She's been living with Rachel for—what? Seven, eight years now? I know it would drive me crazy, too. Why, just the other afternoon, Theda Duckworth and I told Jessica it was high time she started stepping out again. Looks like today's the day. I can hardly wait.

It's a good thing I've got Rachel's number on speed dial. Now, if you'll excuse me...

Dear Reader,

We just knew you wouldn't want to miss the news event that has all of Wyoming abuzz! There's a herd of eligible bachelors on their way to Lightning Creek—and they're all for sale!

Cowboy, park ranger, rancher, P.I.—they all grew up at Lost Springs Ranch, and every one of these mavericks has his price, so long as the money's going to help keep Lost Springs afloat.

The auction is about to begin! Young and old, every woman in the state wants in on the action, so pony up some cash and join the fun. The man of your dreams might just be up for grabs!

Marsha Zinberg
Editorial Coordinator, HEART OF THE WEST

THE RANCHER AND THE RICH GIRL
Heather MacAllister

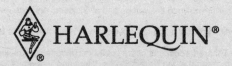

TORONTO • NEW YORK • LONDON
AMSTERDAM • PARIS • SYDNEY • HAMBURG
STOCKHOLM • ATHENS • TOKYO • MILAN • MADRID
PRAGUE • WARSAW • BUDAPEST • AUCKLAND

Heather MacAllister is acknowledged as the author of this work.

ISBN 0-373-82591-9

THE RANCHER AND THE RICH GIRL

Visit us at www.romance.net

Printed in U.S.A.

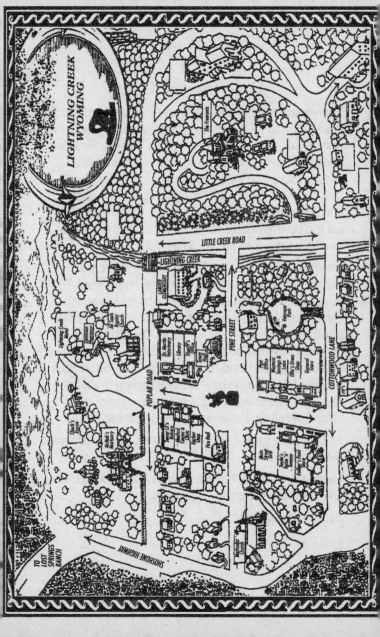

A Note from the Author

Even though I live in the largest city in Texas, small family ranches are all around us. Ranchers have struggled in the past several years, particularly against drought. Some have given up. Others have adapted. Both my sons attend schools located on parcels of former ranch land, and in fact, the ranches are still there. The cows don't seem to mind summer marching band practice or fall football. And not too far from where I live, there's a ranch that's now a game preserve. That got me thinking....

We were in the Jeep, hearing the lecture about how irritable a rhinoceros can be, when the Jeep stalled. The rhinos wandered closer. We were instructed to remain quiet—and no sudden movements. The cowhand (rhino hand?) in charge whipped out his walkie-talkie and informed someone of his situation, then complained loudly that herding rhinos and "other critters" was not what he felt his life's calling to be. After transferring to another Jeep, and subsequently being spit on by a camel and chased by zebras, I understood this sentiment exactly.

My boys had a great time, but then again, they ducked when the camel spit.

I hope you enjoy reading *The Rancher and the Rich Girl*. And there are no camels—I promise.

Heather MacAllister

Dedicated with Alpha Gam love to
Betty Leatherwood Adams, and her daughters
Carroll Ann and Diana Adams McNeill,
who each own a complete collection of my books.

CHAPTER ONE

"I JUST GOT BACK from Lost Springs—I wanted to make sure the extra bleachers are all ready for the auction this weekend." Jessica Fremont cradled the telephone between her ear and her shoulder as she fixed her son, Sam, a peanut butter and banana sandwich on whole-wheat bread for an after-school snack.

"You've been a real lifesaver, Jessica," her friend Lauren DeVane said breezily. "Lindsay will be forever in your debt. I hope Fremont Construction's generosity is going to be mentioned during the auction."

"Not to worry. Lindsay's already given us a full-page ad in the brochure."

"I know, but it doesn't hurt to keep donors happy," Lauren replied. "Lindsay must be thrilled at all the support she's received. Who would have believed a bachelor auction in Wyoming would generate so much good will? I'm really glad I've been able to play even a little part."

Jessica knew that Lauren's "little part" involved a substantial financial contribution to their friend Lindsay's auction.

Underneath her polished veneer, Lauren had a well-developed social conscience and had worked hard for a lot of good causes on the charity circuit. At one time, Jessica had been headed in that direction herself.

And then one snowy day, on a ski slope in Switzerland, she'd met one Samuel Fremont from Lightning Creek, Wyoming, fallen madly in love and that was that. Just over a year of absolute bliss had followed before...

But that was nearly nine years ago. "Lindsay is a saint to take on running that boys' ranch after her parents died," Jessica said. "And now that her uncle's retired, it can't be easy for her, though she'd never say so."

"Oh, I know, but truly good people make me nervous. Listen, I have another favor, which is actually why I called."

Jessica smiled to herself as she screwed the top back onto the peanut butter jar. Lauren's almost fiancé was going to be one of the bachelors auctioned. Since Lauren wasn't going to be at the auction, Jessica had been expecting a request for her to bid on him.

"Liz and Tara promised to come to the auction and someplace called the Starlite is full. Is the Starlite the *only* hotel in Lightning Creek?"

"Actually, it's more of a motel."

"Well, there you are then," Lauren said, as though everything were settled. "They'll have to stay with you."

Liz and Tara, the McNeil sisters. Jessica shifted the phone to her other ear as she got the milk jug out of the refrigerator. She, Lauren and the McNeils had been roommates at school before Jessica had dropped out to get married at nineteen. Jessica hadn't seen them for a long time—since her husband Samuel's funeral in fact. She hadn't seen any of her old friends but Lauren since then—and that was only because Lauren had made the effort.

Liz and Tara...how many times had they nearly been

expelled because they were out after curfew? Jessica tried to imagine them here. "I don't know, Lauren. We live awfully quietly."

There was a potent silence. "Jessica, I'm going to be frank."

Jessica rolled her eyes. Lauren was never less than frank.

"Liz and Tara would be doing you a favor. You've spent *years* holed up in the middle of nowhere with your kid and your mother-in-law. It's…it's not *natural*. We've all been talking about how you've become so drearily domestic—"

"Drearily domestic?"

"Admit it. In your wildest nightmares, did you ever think your life would turn out the way it has?"

"I'm not unhappy, Lauren."

"You're not anything."

"I beg your pardon!"

Lauren laughed. "You just need a good shaking up, and since you won't come to us, I'm going to send Liz and Tara to you. You can thank me by bidding on one of the bachelors for yourself. Maybe even my Rob…wait, have you put on any weight since I've seen you last?"

"No."

"Then you better not bid on him. He really likes the tall, slender, blond type."

"Lauren!" Jessica laughed in spite of herself.

"I know, I'm being ridiculous, except about Liz and Tara. Can they stay with you?"

"I don't know," Jessica hedged. She *did* need a good shaking up.

"Come on, Jessica, you'll love having them there.

Remember when we were in school and we'd stay up all night in each others' rooms?''

"And fall asleep during morning assembly, yes."

"It sounds like such fun, I'm almost sorry I'll be in the Bay Area, but I've had this trip planned for ages."

Sam would be home from school soon, so Jessica was going to have to cut Lauren off in a minute. After-school snacktime was her special time with Sam, and nobody and nothing, except soccer practice, interfered.

"Now give me directions to your house so I can tell them," Lauren said.

Jessica hesitated. "I should check with Rachel. I can't just spring houseguests on my mother-in-law."

"It'll be good for her, too."

Lauren was right. They could stand a little variation in their routine. And the auction was the only event on the calendar this weekend.

Rachel shouldn't object. Jessica knew that the Fremonts used to have house parties all the time. In fact, as she understood it, that had been the point of building such a huge house in tiny Lightning Creek to begin with.

"Come on, Jessica," Lauren urged softly. "It'll only be for a couple of days."

Jessica capped the milk jug and looked out the window on her way back to the refrigerator. "Let me think about it," she said as she caught the blur of yellow through the trees—her signal that the school bus had dropped Sam off at the end of the long driveway.

"While you're thinking, think about how it will look if Liz and Tara come all that way and *don't* stay with you."

Lauren had a point. "Okay," Jessica agreed with some of her old impulsiveness, and was surprised to find she was already looking forward to seeing her friends again.

They decided Jessica would call the McNeils herself, and the next thing Jessica knew, Lauren had hung up, leaving her with the telephone in one hand, the milk jug in another and houseguests coming in less than forty-eight hours.

"Mom!" The door slammed open as Sam burst in, shed his backpack, kicked his shoes across the foyer and headed for the kitchen. "I'm hungry! What have we got to eat?"

"Peanut butter and banana." Jessica pushed the impending house party to the back of her mind and put the milk away.

"Aw, Mom." Sam slid across the tile in his stockinged feet and slouched into a chair. "Gramma lets me have pizza pockets."

"Too much fat and too many additives," Jessica replied automatically. Putting the sandwich and milk in front of him, she sat at the table.

Drearily domestic or not, Jessica lived for these few minutes as Sam wolfed down his snack and babbled about his day. Then he'd go upstairs or over to a friend's house to play, and Jessica would return to her office at Fremont Construction until dinnertime. The end of the school year would soon be here and she knew she'd miss the routine.

Sam swallowed half the milk and swiped at his mouth. "Kevin is going to go to sleep-away camp. He's going to learn how to ride horses, and then when he gets back, his parents are getting him a horse! I want to go to that camp. Then when you and Gramma see how good I can ride, it would be stupid not to get me a horse, too."

It was an old argument and Jessica was running out of excuses. Rachel had forbidden Sam to own a horse and, secretly, Jessica had been relieved not to have the responsibility of making the decision herself. In the past when she'd refused him, she had pointed out how much time and energy a horse would require and that Sam wasn't old enough to be able to give the animal that kind of care. She had a feeling that this time the excuse wouldn't work.

"Sam…" she began gently.

"Kevin is three months and six days younger than me! He's getting a horse—why can't *I* have a horse?"

Because your father was killed on a horse and your grandmother and I don't want the same thing to happen to you. But she couldn't say that to a nine-year-old. She didn't even like admitting it to herself because she knew she'd grown too safe, too bland. Too predictable. "I'll talk to Gramma about it, okay?"

A voice sounded from the mudroom. "Talk to Gramma about what?" Rachel came through the back door of the kitchen.

"Me getting a horse!"

Rachel met Jessica's eyes and a look passed between the two women. "His friend Kevin is going to a riding camp this summer," Jessica explained. "Sam thinks it's something he would like to do, too."

"And a horse afterward!" Even muffled by peanut butter, Sam's voice sounded shrill.

Rachel carefully placed her purse on the telephone table and picked up the stack of mail Jessica had dropped there earlier. "Horses are very large animals, Sam. They're dangerous—"

"Kevin's parents don't think so!"

She looked at him, her expression revealing the grief she still felt. "Kevin's father didn't—"

"That wasn't the horse's fault! You said it was the camera flash that scared him!"

"Sam, stop interrupting your grandmother." Jessica wanted to head off Rachel, too. Her mother-in-law's face had paled and the letters she held quivered in her hands.

Sam visibly gathered himself, then said with determination, "I want a horse." He raised his chin just the slightest bit, and Jessica was instantly reminded of his father saying to Rachel, "I want to marry Jessica."

"No," Rachel said now, just as she'd said then.

"I'm going to be a cowboy and own a ranch like my father. I need a horse."

"You are not going to be a cowboy. Fremonts are not cowboys."

"Then I don't want to be a Fremont!" Sam's face reddened. "I never get to do *anything!* You treat me like a baby! I hate you—both of you!" Shoving back the chair, he bolted from the table.

Jessica was so shocked she could only stare after him. His footsteps thudded up the stairs, across the landing and into his room. The door slammed. The last time a door had been slammed in the Fremont mansion, Jessica herself had done it.

She'd been angry at Rachel then, too.

Now she looked apologetically at the woman who'd become her partner in raising Sam. "I—he's never…I'll go talk to him."

"Wait and let him cool off."

Jessica was surprised. After Sam's outburst, she would have expected Rachel to follow him upstairs and deliver a lecture on the proper behavior for Fremonts.

Controlling emotions was a basic tenet of the Fremont family.

During the early weeks of her marriage, Jessica had struggled to subdue her natural spontaneity and to think carefully before she spoke. Being a member of a wealthy family with political aspirations meant any off-hand remarks might end up out of context in the newspaper. It had been difficult for her, but until now, she hadn't believed her son had inherited any of her volatility, as Rachel had once referred to her temper.

"Are you all right?" she asked her mother-in-law.

Rachel nodded and scanned the mail. "He's a lot like his father."

He was? Jessica had never heard her husband raise his voice.

"I think we ought to send him to camp with his friend," she suggested. "Maybe he won't like horses. He's bound to get tired of caring for them. This whole cowboy thing is probably a phase, anyway. I mean, every other boy his age is playing computer games."

"No," Rachel said. "He will go to Marshallfield Day Camp as usual. He'll meet boys from good families there. He'll form lifelong friendships that will provide a network of support for him in the future."

She sounded like the brochure, Jessica thought. Probably because Rachel had written the brochure thirty years earlier.

Sam's father had attended Marshallfield. Now that Jessica thought about it, her husband hadn't ever spoken of good old Marshallfield and the wonderful memories it held for him.

Something in the tone of Rachel's voice and the way she spoke grated on Jessica, but she didn't want to argue now.

"Lauren DeVane called me a few minutes ago," she said, deliberately changing the subject.

"Dare I hope it had nothing to do with that vulgar auction?"

"No." Jessica hid a smile by turning to clear away the remains of Sam's snack.

Rachel chaired the annual Lightning Creek Ladies Auxiliary fund drive. The Lost Springs Ranch for Boys was one of the recipients that split the modest amount raised each year. Lindsay, the ranch's owner, and Rex Trowbridge, the director, had enlisted outside help in planning the auction and there were obviously still ruffled feathers.

"Liz and Tara McNeil will be in town for the auction and Lauren thought it would be fun if they could stay here." Closing the dishwasher, Jessica added, "It's been years since I've seen them. I'm looking forward to it." She reached for the hand towel.

Rachel was silent. Jessica glanced at her as she hung up the towel and saw that the older woman's lips were pressed in a grim line. "It's out of the question."

A pang of disappointment shot through Jessica. "Why?"

"Surely I don't have to tell you."

The past ten years evaporated and Jessica once again felt like the new bride eager to please her stern mother-in-law.

"I don't understand what's wrong with them staying here," she said. "We've certainly got the room."

"It isn't appropriate," Rachel pronounced in a low voice.

"Why not? You used to have house parties all the time!"

"That was…before."

Now Jessica understood. Walking over to Rachel, she put her arm around the older woman's shoulder. "It's been nearly nine years since Sam and his father died, Rachel, though I know it sometimes seems like yesterday. Just because I want to see a couple of my friends doesn't mean that I'm forgetting Samuel."

Rachel stiffened and Jessica dropped her arm. "I should hope not. As a Fremont, you have certain obligations."

Jessica stepped back. "Supporting this auction is one of those obligations, isn't it?"

"You've supported it plenty."

"I know." Jessica waited, her expression as Fremont-like as she could make it.

Rachel scrutinized her, then nodded slightly. "Have your friends here, if you must. But, Jessica, do try to maintain some decorum. Remember, you're a Fremont."

Jessica hadn't been reminded that she was a Fremont in quite a while and was irritated that Rachel did so now. Hadn't she proved herself yet? "I'm aware of my responsibilities and one of them is upstairs, very upset that he can't have a horse."

Rachel shot her a sharp look. "I'm surprised you can even contemplate it."

But Jessica *was* contemplating it. This was the latest in a series of escalating disagreements between her and her mother-in-law on how to raise Sam, and it was by far the biggest. The others were small—just differences of style mostly. Like the high-fat snacks Rachel let Sam eat more often than Jessica thought was reasonable. She yielded on that, as she did on most issues when it came to Sam. After all, Rachel was more experienced. She'd raised Sam's father, the man Jessica had fallen in love with.

"Let's at least look into this camp that he wants to go to," Jessica suggested. "I'm going upstairs to talk with him."

Her footsteps sounded loud as they crossed the polished wooden floors to the grand double staircase with the banisters and railings carved by local craftsmen. The designs didn't match, though they were all carved from ponderosa pine. Ever mindful of potential votes, Samuel's father had used more than one local carver. At first, Jessica had thought it too obviously political. Now she liked the differing styles.

As she reached the top of the stairs, her footsteps slowed. It was past time she returned to work, but she didn't want to leave Sam while he was angry.

She knocked on his bedroom door and waited, not expecting an answer. She didn't get one. Turning the knob, she pushed open the door. "Sam?"

"Go away." He was standing by his dresser. On the top, framed in rough wood with barbed wire embedded in it, was a photograph of his father and grandfather, dressed in fancy Western outfits and sitting on their horses as they prepared to ride in the Frontier Days parade.

Jessica walked over to join him, encouraged when he didn't tell her to go away again. "No promises, but I'll talk to Gramma."

Sam gave her a bleak look. "She'll just make me go to Marshallfield."

As she stared into the unhappy face of her son, Jessica felt as though she were awakening after a long sleep.

She'd been raising Sam in the same house with the

same woman and the same experiences that had molded her late husband—the man she'd fallen in love with. He even had the same name. *My God,* she thought. *Rachel is raising her son all over again. Only Sam is my son, too.*

But Jessica had liked this environment for her son. She had grown up without a sense of where "home" was. Her father, a surgeon, had invented a type of clamp that temporarily stopped blood flow without as much tissue damage as its predecessor. He'd traveled all over the world, accompanied by Jessica and her mother, demonstrating the clamp and lecturing at medical schools. Until she'd gone to boarding school, Jessica had had a private tutor who'd traveled with them. Even after she went to boarding school—because her mother wanted her to have the opportunity to make friendships that lasted longer than a few weeks—Jessica hadn't realized how different her childhood was, since many of the other students had parents who lived and worked in other countries, or traveled like Jessica's.

It was only after holiday visits to friends' homes that she experienced a taste of what she now thought of as a real home life.

The Fremonts had a real home life. She'd been impressed with how deep their roots were in Wyoming. When faced with raising her son without his father, she'd tried for the next best thing—raising him in the same house with the same woman.

Had she made a huge mistake by living with her mother-in-law and allowing her such a big role in rearing Sam all these years?

"Tell you what. I've got to go back to work now, but this evening, I'll call Kevin's mother, and if I like the sound of the camp, then I'll sign you up," she promised recklessly.

After all, *she* was Sam's mother, not Rachel.

CHAPTER TWO

"SO YOU'RE REALLY GOIN' through with it?"

"I'm really going through with it." Matt Winston closed the door of the horse trailer and patted the rump of Black Star, his best horse.

"You're gonna regret it."

Matt glanced at Frank—aka the Flying Francisco—and nodded. "Probably."

"I know it. Carmen read the tea leaves this morning."

"I had coffee."

Frank gestured dismissively. "So maybe it was coffee grounds. No matter. I'm tellin' you that this trip will not be as you expect."

"Things rarely are." Matt didn't know whether Frank was referring to the sale of Black Star, or Matt driving from his ranch in Texas to Wyoming to take part in the bachelor auction at Lost Springs Ranch for Boys this weekend. Didn't matter. Matt would likely regret both.

"On the other hand, they say regrets are the spice of goulash."

"Do they?"

Frank shrugged, causing the capuchin monkey perched on his shoulder to shift and curl its tail. "They do in the old country."

Privately Matt thought the old country was some

place like New Jersey, but he'd never called Frank on it. "What do they say about bachelor auctions?"

Squinting, Frank stared off into the distance. "They say being a rich woman's play toy is nice work if you can get it, but keep your own horse in the stable."

Matt grinned. "It's just a date in return for a donation to Lost Springs."

"Yeah, yeah, for charity. Homeless boys like you once were. I know all this." Frank nodded toward the trailer. "And the horse?"

Matt's smile faded as he rubbed the animal again. "There are going to be people with money at this auction. Black Star will fetch a better price than if I tried to sell him from here."

"Barnaby would not sell an animal he wanted to keep. He'd just spend a coin. Right, Caesar?" Frank fed a nut to the monkey.

A coin? It would take a lot of coins to keep Winter Ranch going. Hundreds. Thousands. Millions would be nice. How had Barnaby Schultz, the late owner, managed? Matt had only inherited the ranch—not the knack for keeping it going on nothing.

Before he came to own Winter Ranch, Barnaby had been a carnival magician. Matt figured he must have been a pretty good one, because magic was about the only explanation he could think of for the way Barnaby had always come up with money when they needed it.

Matt sure couldn't—at least not the extra to support the former circus animals who were just living out their final days.

Caesar chattered and there was an answering growl from the shade beneath the big pecan tree in the ranch yard.

"How're you doing, Sheba?" he called to the old

tiger. At the same time, Frank barked a command in some language the animals understood, but Matt didn't.

"They see you putting Black Star in the trailer and think we are getting ready to move like in the old days," Frank said. In the distance an elephant trumpeted.

Matt noted that the sound was closer than it should have been and shot Frank a questioning glance.

"You're upsetting the animals," Frank warned. "And, hey, you're gonna need a horse. Where are you gonna find a horse who's friends with them, eh?"

"Selling Black Star isn't my first choice, just my best one." Matt's jaw tightened as he tested the latch on the trailer. "It appears that Barnaby spent all the 'coins' you keep telling me about."

Frank's handlebar moustache quivered and he gave Matt a dark look from beneath heavy black brows. "Nothing was said of this."

Frank looked very much like Francisco at the moment. The closest thing to a foreman that Matt had, Frank had acted as the liaison between the ranch hands and the circus folk who'd traditionally wintered at the far northeast corner of the Hill Country ranch. Only somewhere along the line, the regular ranch hands had drifted away and the retired circus folk had become the ranch folk. Frank's accent changed according to which hat he was wearing at the time.

"Nothing much to say. There wasn't a lot of money in the ranch account when Barnaby died. There's less now." Matt gave Black Star a last reassuring pat and headed toward the door of his truck until a chattering interrupted him. Right. He'd said the word *coin* a few moments ago.

Caesar leaped down from Frank's shoulder and scurried toward Matt. The monkey turned around once, gave a funny hop and held out a tiny hand.

Matt searched the pockets of his well-worn jeans. "You used to dance a lot longer than that, Caesar."

"He's gettin' old like the rest of us." Frank was back to being Frank.

Matt finally found a nickel and handed it to the monkey. Caesar snatched the coin, bit it, chattered some more, then scampered away until he came to the base of the pecan tree, where Sheba yawned at him. He turned around, saw Matt and Frank watching him and let loose with a stream of monkey chatter. They turned away and Caesar ran off to who knew where.

"Maybe I should hit Caesar up for a loan," Matt said only half kidding. After Barnaby died, Caesar had relentlessly pestered Matt for coins. The monkey might be worth more than he was, he thought.

"No, no, Matthew," Frank said, his voice slow and deep. "Approach your rich lady—maybe after your date, eh?"

"No." Matt bent to pick up his duffel bag and tossed it into the back of his pickup.

"No?"

"Definitely no." Out of the corner of his eye, Matt saw Frank shrug philosophically.

"What kind of date you got planned, anyway?"

"Well, if she doesn't have her own ideas, I thought I'd get one of those fancy hotels in Casper to pack us a picnic lunch and take her riding through some of the prettiest country God created." With luck, she'd be a horsewoman and would be impressed with Black Star, impressed enough to buy him.

Matt felt a pang at the prospect, even though Black Star was mostly vanity, anyway. The colt had been a gift from Barnaby when Matt had arrived at the ranch straight from Lost Springs. The horse was the offspring of one of the black Hungarian performing high-steppers and ranch stock. Barnaby used to say he liked the fire that the circus horses added to the breeding, but they needed the stability of the ranch horses to settle down and make a really fine animal.

Matt would miss him.

"A picnic," Frank repeated thoughtfully. "With a soft blanket underneath a shady tree and a little vino…" He pursed his lips. "Could work. And afterward—"

"There'll be no afterward!"

"Women expect afterward. You young men today know nothing of how to woo a woman."

"Wooing's got nothing to do with it. I won't even know her. It's only a date!"

"No." Frank held up a finger and shook his head. "You must make it an *event*. I saw the brochure. The ladies, they will be buying a fantasy, you know?"

Matt had seen the brochure, too. The former Lost Springs boys had done well—at least the ones returning to help out at the auction. He'd thought long and hard about going back to the ranch where he'd spent his adolescence. It wasn't that he hated the place—he could see now that living there had been the best thing for him and he definitely wanted to see it keep going for other boys. The second thoughts came when he'd seen the printing proof of the brochure. The other guys had worked hard—real hard. Some were doctors, a couple were ranchers. One of them even owned a toy company.

There was nothing like a reunion to make a man take stock of his life and see how he measured up. Matt supposed he looked more successful on paper than he actually was. On the other hand, he guessed it all came down to how a person defined success. He considered himself successful in the ways that counted—all the people and animals that depended on him had a home and food to eat. And right now, Lost Springs was depending on him to help them. Matt always responded to a plea for help, but this was different. He owed Lost Springs a debt he could never repay.

Frank was still going on about the date part. Truth to tell, Matt hadn't given as much thought to what happened *after* someone bid on him at the auction as he should have, considering that his dating skills were as rusty as the siding on the storage barn. "So…you think the picnic idea is fantasy enough?"

"It's what you make of it, eh?"

"What do you mean?"

"Ninety percent is all up here." Frank tapped his temple. "Dreams, fantasies, desires, endless possibilities—all up here. Most men know they must pleasure a woman's body, but a great lover also pleasures her mind."

This was too much information. "Well now, Frank, you see, it's not—"

"In my prime, the ladies looked fondly upon me." Frank stood straighter and threw back his shoulders. "And even after the fall—" he swiped at his lame leg "—my upper body was *molto bene,* you know? From the trapeze catching. You…you are not so bad—not for trapeze work, you understand, but not bad for the ladies. You have good shoulders and your belly is not so much in evidence." Frank laughed and patted his slight paunch. "You will draw many eyes."

Matt hoped he'd draw many bids. He tilted his hat further down on his head. "Yeah, well, it's about time for me to take off here."

"They like the quiet ones who watch them. You are good at this." Frank crossed his arms over his still-massive chest and narrowed his eyes at Matt. "Yes. You pick one or two ladies and you look at them as though they are the only women in the room. Look fully into their eyes—let me see you look into my eyes."

Matt winced. "Frank—"

"Look."

Matt looked.

"No...*look*. Like so." Frank gave him a look that made Matt glad he didn't have any sisters to protect.

"Notice the smile." Frank gestured. "Just a slight movement of the lips. You are making the promise, no?"

"I don't make promises I can't keep," Matt muttered.

"Matthew, Matthew." Frank's accent thickened and he attempted to throw his arm around Matt's shoulders. Matt was considerably taller, so all Frank managed was a heavy pat.

There was still a lot of power in his arms, Matt realized.

"You have promised your time, and the lady who wins you expects to receive all your attention. You must make her believe that you will think only of her, that you find her utterly fascinating—that you are content merely being near her, and your only thoughts will be those of how to please her." Frank spread his hand, indicating a vista of possibilities. "She must be convinced that she is your only reason for living."

"All that from a look and a smile?"

"Think of yourself as a character in a play. You both know it will end, for a brief time you are together—or a longer time, who knows, eh?'' He poked Matt in the ribs. ''Maybe you won't come back to us here.''

''I'm not going to run out on you.'' Even Matt heard the harshness in his voice.

Frank regarded him thoughtfully. ''If you don't want to come back here, then you shouldn't.''

Matt looked at him in genuine surprise. ''Who said I didn't want to come back here?''

''I only meant that if you find a path that leads you in a different direction, then you should follow it.'' Frank waved his arm to encompass the ranch yard, the barn and outbuildings and the rolling hills in the distance. ''Not much opportunity for a different life comes your way here.''

''I don't want a different life.''

''You came here as a young man. You don't know what you want.''

''All I ever wanted was a place I could set down roots and call my own.''

''And Barnaby took advantage of that. He should have never left you the ranch—and in such a way.'' Frank shook his head. ''You should sell it. No one would blame you.''

But Matt would blame himself. He wasn't sure of all the legal mumbo jumbo, but the bottom line was that the circus people had a lease on their section as long as he owned the ranch. That was a condition of the inheritance. Selling would be a complicated process that would void the lease. And truthfully, finding a buyer who'd put up with the eccentricities of having retired circus performers wandering around the ranch was about nil. ''I couldn't do that to you.''

''What makes you think we can't take care of ourselves, eh? A little snow on the roof doesn't mean you can't see out the windows.''

"What does that mean?"

"It means that while you're entertaining your rich lady, you might find you like it and want to stay. So stay. Enjoy yourself. We'll be okay without you.''

Matt had his doubts, but appreciated Frank's gesture.

Caesar chose that moment to come bounding back and climb onto Frank's shoulder.

"It's getting past time for me to shove off,'' Matt said.

"Lita packed you lunch?''

"Yeah.'' Before climbing into the pickup truck, Matt turned and waved toward the kitchen window where the gruff ex-carnival cook stood watching.

Frank and Caesar leaned in the truck. ''Don't do anything I wouldn't do,'' Frank said, then added with a jovial bellow, ''Fortunately, there isn't much I wouldn't do!''

Matt grinned good-naturedly, put the truck in gear and drove off, leaving the ranch in the hands of a lame trapeze artist and a money-hungry monkey.

"JESSICA!'' The two brunettes on the doorstep threw their arms around Jessica and squeezed. Their hugs felt as though they were squeezing life back into her.

"It's good to see you, Liz, Tara,'' Jessica said, hugging them back.

"So when are you breaking out the margaritas?''

"In the middle of the afternoon?''

"Jessica, Jessica.'' Shaking her head, Tara picked up a hanging garment bag. ''Have you forgotten that there's never a bad time for margaritas?''

Well yes, she had. Feeling vaguely improper—margaritas weren't normally a Fremont drink—Jessica mixed a pitcher of the frozen slush and carried it into the den.

It took no time at all to become reacquainted with her two friends. References to people, places and events whirled around her, and Jessica began to feel a longing for a way of life she'd happily abandoned nearly a decade ago. She was also forced to admit just how staid and circumscribed she'd become—maybe even boring. Okay, *probably* boring. At the very least, predictable. Jessica had never been predictable when she'd been in school with Tara and Liz.

"Where's your baby?" Liz asked Jessica.

"He's nine now."

"No way!"

"Has it been *that* long since you eloped?" Tara asked.

"I didn't elope," Jessica protested. "I just had a small wedding."

"I guess *so*. One minute you were next to me on the ski slope, and the next, you were in a lip lock with this gorgeous man," Liz said.

"Yeah, and then a week later, Lauren was packing up your stuff at school and telling us you'd dropped out to get married," Tara recalled. "You always were impulsive."

"Then the next thing you know, there was the pitter-patter of tiny feet—you really jumped into things, didn't you?" Liz was as blunt as always.

"Well…I got pregnant on our honeymoon," Jessica explained. "We went on a cruise and I was so seasick that I kept throwing up my birth control pills." She realized she'd never told anyone this before.

Tara grinned. "You must not have been seasick *all* the time."

"We spent two weeks on St. Thomas, but after we got back, I kept wondering why the seasickness wouldn't go away!" When the laughter faded, Jessica added, "But I'm glad it happened that way. If we'd waited..." She couldn't finish.

She didn't have to. Liz got to her first, enveloping her in a hug. "I'm so sorry, Jessie. Life stinks sometimes."

"I realize Samuel's been gone a long time, but seeing you again reminds me of that last time we were all together in Switzerland and I first met him." Jessica managed a wobbly smile. "But don't feel sorry for me. I got the best little boy in the world out of the deal, so I'm happy."

"Well, where is he?" Tara asked, breaking the somber atmosphere.

"In school until three-thirty." A good thing, too. Jessica had been so busy with preparations for her houseguests that Sam had been feeling neglected and had let her know it. To be fair, he was used to having the undivided attention of both his mother and grandmother.

"In that case..." Tara kicked off her shoes and dug out the auction brochure. "Plenty of time to figure out who we're bidding on!" She patted the spot next to her on the sofa. Jessica joined her.

"What's this *we* business?" Liz opened the brochure and pointed to a man wearing a tuxedo and holding a rose. "I plan to get Rob, here, all for myself."

"*Lauren's* Rob? Are you nuts?" Tara had always been a little intimidated by Lauren.

"That'll teach her not to show up."

Tara took a sip of her drink and shook her head. "Give me a man in tight jeans anytime."

"We've got a couple of those in here." Liz flipped through the brochure. "Look, here's a cowboy—hey, a rodeo champion." She read the brief profile out loud.

Tara turned the page in her copy of the brochure. "I was kinda looking at this one with the horse." She showed Jessica.

Jessica stared down into an unsmiling face half-hidden by a cowboy hat. The man was standing next to a striking black horse with an irregularly shaped white splotch on its forehead.

Although she'd glanced through the brochure, Jessica wasn't going to bid on anyone, so she hadn't studied the men who were to participate in the auction. And as soon as she'd seen the horse in this photo, she'd quickly flipped past.

Samuel's horse had been dark with white markings—not as black as this one appeared to be, but enough like it to make Jessica uncomfortable. She'd never been a horsewoman, though she'd vowed to learn to ride well for her husband's sake, but that had never happened.

"He looks like the strong, silent type," Tara said. "One who lets his actions speak for him. My kind of man."

Liz reached for the brochure. "I thought you were talking about the horse."

"Oh, ha ha."

"How about you, Jessie?" Liz fanned the pages of the brochure. "Which one are you bidding on?"

Smiling, Jessica shook her head. "Oh, I'm not going to bid."

"Why not?"

"Because…because…I guess it never occurred to me to bid on one of the bachelors."

"Again, why not?"

"Well…"

"There are some *prime* specimens in that brochure," Tara said.

"Jessie, you should bid on one of these guys," her sister added.

Jessica mentally tested the idea. "Well, what on earth would I do with him afterward?"

"Ain't that just the saddest thing you've ever heard?" Tara drawled.

"You can't be *that* rusty," Liz teased.

Jessica could and was. "You know, between learning the ins and outs of the construction business and raising my son, I haven't had the emotional energy to go looking for a new relationship."

"That's why this auction is so perfect," Tara said. "You pay your money and you have control. The men agree to do what you want."

Liz poured the last of the margaritas into her glass. "I like the sound of that."

"You know what I mean," Tara said. "The auction is a great way to get your feet wet again. Let's find you a bachelor. How about page thirty-four—the park ranger?"

"Sounds like a loner-type," was Liz's opinion. "Try for something more urban. Page twenty-eight is a cutie."

"So's twelve."

They continued going through the brochure, making more and more outrageous comments about the men. Jessica found herself laughing so much the muscles in her cheeks were sore. She still had no intention of bidding on one of the auction bachelors—Rachel would have a cow—but she was having a good time, anyway.

Having the McNeils here showed her as nothing else could that she'd neglected the "Jessica" part of herself. Maybe she should bid on one of the bachelors after all.

"I could hear raucous laughter all the way from the back driveway." From the doorway, Rachel's voice rolled like a fog over the group, dampening their spirits.

"Rachel." Jessica stumbled as she got to her feet. She'd been sitting so long her leg was partially asleep, but Rachel's silent gaze had already noted the empty margarita pitcher. "I'd like you to meet my friends." Jessica quickly introduced the McNeil sisters. Rachel acknowledged them with a frosty Fremont smile of disapproval, which they ignored.

"So, Mrs. Fremont, which of these gorgeous hunks will you be bidding on?" Liz asked, waving the brochure.

"I will not be attending the auction," Rachel pronounced in a tone that managed to convey to everyone that she felt Jessica shouldn't be attending, either.

"Good," Liz said. "I was afraid you'd run up the price on the toy boy."

"Liz!" Even Tara was surprised at her sister.

"Amos Pike owns a toy company," Liz said mildly, but with the unrepentant twinkle Jessica remembered so well.

"Rachel, you're home early today," she interjected before Liz could say anything more.

"It's four o'clock," her mother-in-law said clearly.

"But it can't be!" Jessica stared at her watch. It *was* four o'clock. She'd lost all track of time. "Oh my God, where's Sam?"

CHAPTER THREE

"YOU MEAN HE'S NOT HOME yet?" Rachel paled.

"I—I—" All the air had left Jessica's lungs.

"Maybe he came in the back door," Liz suggested. "He probably saw us all in here and went up to his room."

Not Sam, Jessica thought. He'd never come home to anything other than his mother or grandmother waiting with a snack.

"Go look, Jessie." Tara nudged her past Rachel.

"Are you telling me you don't know where your own son is?" Rachel's voice echoed with condemnation.

Jessica hurried toward the stairs. "He's probably in his room." She hoped.

But when Jessica saw the door slightly ajar, she knew Sam wasn't in there. Still, she opened the door all the way and took in the smooth bedspread, which meant he hadn't flung himself onto his bed since this morning.

She stood there, mentally reviewing Sam's schedule. Was there a rehearsal for some end-of-the-school-year program she'd forgotten? Spring soccer had finished two weeks ago and the summer season didn't begin until school let out.

"Call Sheriff Hatcher." Rachel had reached the top of the stairs.

"Sam's only a half-hour late," Jessica murmured, well aware that her friends were listening while they pretended not to. "He probably went to Kevin's house."

"Without telling you? Do you allow this behavior?"

Jessica looked at her mother-in-law and tried to infuse her voice with a calm she was rapidly losing. "No, Rachel, but the circumstances are a little different this week. Let's not panic before we've made a few phone calls." She started down the stairs.

Rachel grasped her arm as Jessica moved past. "This town is packed with strangers in for that...*auction*. Anything could have happened to him."

Jessica didn't reply.

Sam wasn't at Kevin's house. There weren't any practices at school. She called the bus barn and was put on hold while the dispatcher radioed the driver, who was now on her high school run.

Though they only lived a short distance from Lander Elementary, Jessica had allowed Sam to take the bus that was available for kids who lived at the outer limits of the town rather than pick him up herself. That way he could enjoy a little independence and she didn't need to worry about his safety. Now she wasn't so sure it was such a good idea.

"How could you, Jessica?" Rachel snapped.

Jessica took a deep breath. "My schedule has been crazy all week. The afternoon just got away from me."

"Your friends have only been here a few hours and look at the influence they've had on you," Rachel went on, her voice loud enough to carry through the kitchen door and be heard by Liz and Tara. "You've forgotten all your responsibilities."

In spite of her worry about Sam, Jessica was concerned about her mother-in-law. This querulousness wasn't like her, and she didn't want Liz and Tara spreading the word that Jessica lived with a dragon. "Please, let's just concentrate on finding Sam."

"And how do you propose to do that?"

At that moment, the transportation dispatcher returned with the information that Sam had been dropped off in his usual spot at the foot of the long driveway leading to the Fremont house, though he'd tried to get off earlier and hadn't been allowed. "Our policy is that any change in a child's routine must be in writing," the woman said.

"Yes, thank you." Slowly Jessica replaced the phone and tried to figure out what to do next.

"Well?"

"They dropped him off just like they always do."

"I'm calling the sheriff." Rachel reached for the phone, but Jessica stayed her hand.

Overreacting wouldn't get them anywhere. She needed to give Rachel some task to take her mind off Sam. "Would you start dinner for me? I've already made the pasta salad and there's a fruit platter in the fridge."

Rachel blinked. "You're acting very calm about all this. Just how much have you had to drink?"

Jessica kept her voice even as she walked across the kitchen. "I had one margarita about three hours ago. I'm fine. Now, let's see…dessert is Chocolate Death brownies from Sweet Lil's." She opened the bread keeper. "So, basically, I just need the French bread heated and the raw vegetables arranged—"

"I can't believe you!" Rachel gestured wildly. "My only grandson is God knows where and you're worried about feeding those women?"

Determined not to give in to Rachel's panic, Jessica withdrew a loaf of bread. "The bus driver said Sam tried to get off before his stop. Something must have caught his attention so I'm going to get in the car and trace the bus route to see if I can find him. You stay here in case he calls." She managed a smile. "Now, put on your Fremont face and pass around the raw veggies."

MATT WOULD BE STAYING at the old Starlite Motel, but planned to board Black Star up at Lost Springs. He'd contacted Rex Trowbridge, a fellow Lost Springs alum who was now the director of the ranch. Rex had said boarding the horse wouldn't be a problem.

Matt had kind of been hoping it would be, so he'd have had an excuse not to bring Black Star. His ranch could get by for a while, but selling Black Star was inevitable. Midsize ranchers were struggling all over the Hill Country after last season's drought, and this year wasn't looking much better.

The thing was, if he was going to have to sell Black Star, he'd get a better price now than later. With his black coat and that Hungarian horse blood in him, Black Star was a showy animal, the kind that brought a good price from people with money.

In Matt's experience, show always brought a higher price than substance.

Still, during the past three days of driving, he'd nearly convinced himself that he could find some other way to keep the ranch afloat.

It had been the signs for the Kingston Wildlife Sanctuary in Texas that had given him the idea of a sponsor. The place was a couple of hundred miles from Winter Ranch and Matt had been passing their advertising signs along the highway. The closer he got, the more detail was on the signs, and then he'd seen the one thanking the sponsors. He'd only caught a few of the names as he'd driven past, but seeing the list of companies and individuals made him wonder why it hadn't ever occurred to him to have some wild animal rescue group contribute to the upkeep of the older performing animals instead of shouldering most of the feed bills himself.

If anyone was running a sanctuary, he was, though it was hardly the model of efficiency.

But he couldn't just let the animals starve. They were all old, and most of them were tame enough to be pets. No zoo wanted them, and Matt shuddered at the thought of turning them over to the big game ranches in the Hill Country.

He prayed he'd never get that desperate.

Matt reached the outskirts of Lightning Creek and passed by the Starlite on Main. Some mighty fine-looking vehicles were parked in the lot already. He doubted the old place had ever seen such expensive cars. A couple of them were probably worth more than the old motel with its flickering Vaca-cy sign. Somebody had hand lettered a big No and duct-taped it just under the blinking star. Good thing he had a reservation.

Since he planned to stop at Reilly's Feed Store to pick up feed for Black Star, Matt headed for the statue of a cowboy on a bucking bronc, which sat in the middle of the traffic circle in the center of town.

He smiled to himself as he passed the statue. How many times had he looked at that statue on a trip into town and dreamed of becoming a famous bronc rider? To his adolescent way of thinking, that was the quickest road to fame and riches and getting back with his mother.

He'd planned to use his winnings to buy a home

where they could live without sneaking away from the landlord. A place all theirs that nobody could take away from them.

The thing of it was, after he'd found out his mother had died, there hadn't seemed to be much point. Yet thanks to old Barnaby, he'd ended up with his own place, anyway. Who'd have thought it?

Matt knew the inheritance hadn't been all altruistic. Barnaby had left him the ranch so he could take care of the people and animals who lived there, and that was fine by Matt. He wouldn't have abandoned them even if Barnaby *hadn't* left him the ranch. Frank and the others were the nearest to a family that he had.

He wasn't going to let them down.

There was the Roadkill Grill. He could still smell the grease-laden air—was anything as good as their fried hamburgers and golden onion rings? He'd have to stop by for dinner after he settled Black Star up at the ranch.

Now, there was a new place—Twyla's Tease 'n' Tweeze. Ruby slippers? The place kind of stuck out, painted pink and all, or maybe it was just because it wasn't part of the Main Street he remembered.

Reilly's Feed Store next door looked the same as ever. Matt had enjoyed the trips into town to get supplies for the ranch.

Three parking spots—two for the feed store and one for the beauty parlor—were free. Matt eased his truck and trailer into all of them, hoping neither establishment had a run of business in the next few minutes.

The traffic light at Pine changed, and he waited until a bright yellow school bus passed by before he got out of the truck and stretched his legs. He watched as the bus headed toward Cottonwood and took a left. It sure was an improvement over the old clunker with the cracked vinyl seats that had bounced him to and from Lost Springs. Some of the boys used to poke holes in the seats with their pencils, but Matt never did. He'd never wanted to break any rules that would get him sent away from the ranch, because then how could his mother find him again?

Shaking his head over the boy he'd been, he walked back to the trailer to check on Black Star.

"Just a little longer," he crooned as he patted him.

A couple coming out of the General Store across the street stared.

A corner of Matt's mouth lifted. He'd traded feed for the horse trailer, which had belonged to one of the circus performing acts. Although he had painted white over the wildly colorful images that pranced all over the sides, the job needed two coats, and Matt had run out of paint. Horses leaping through flaming hoops or being ridden around the show ring by spangled women wearing more feathers than anything else were still visible as ghostly images through the paint.

In a way they were ghosts.

Matt lifted his hand to the couple, who waved back, but still stared. Then he pushed open the door to the feed store and felt as if he were stepping back in time.

Mr. Reilly hadn't changed the layout—in fact, Mr. Reilly himself hadn't changed much. A little grayer, maybe, but he was still parked behind the counter and still wore plaid shirts—flannel in the winter, cotton in the summer, if Matt remembered correctly.

A vaguely familiar-looking younger man was leaning against the glass—something Matt and the other boys hadn't ever been allowed to do. Both he and Mr. Reilly turned when the cowbell on the door clanked.

"Hi, Mr. Reilly. I'm Matt Winston." Matt approached with his hand outstretched. "Remember me?"

"Matt—the responsible one. Sure, I remember you." Mr. Reilly grasped his hand. "How have you been?"

As Matt shook hands with Mr. Reilly, the other man smiled.

"Matt, I'm Rex Trowbridge. Good to see you again. And thanks for coming to the auction."

"No problem." Matt had thought that's who he was, but since Rex had been several grades ahead of him, Matt hadn't known him well. "Hey, it's lucky I ran into you. I was on my way out to Lost Springs with Black Star. Thought I'd stop by here first and get some feed."

Rex gestured around them. "This is the place, as I'm sure you remember."

"Yeah, I do."

"So you brought your horse?" Mr. Reilly asked as he came out from behind the counter. "If it's the one with you in the auction brochure, he's a mighty fine-looking animal."

"That he is." Matt swallowed. "I'm thinking of selling him, if either of you know anybody who might be interested."

He got the words out without choking. So far, so good.

"I saw that picture, too," Rex said. "Lost Springs can always use a good horse, but we're tight on funds just now."

Tell me about it, Matt thought.

"Donating a horse like that would give you a good tax write-off."

The silence that followed Rex's smooth request seemed to stretch forever. Matt was taken aback until he remembered that Rex was a director of the ranch and getting donations was his job. Now he had to figure out a way to refuse Rex without offending him or embarrassing himself.

"I'll be sure and mention the tax advantages to the person who buys Black Star," he replied, hoping Rex wouldn't pursue his request.

He didn't.

"Well, let's get you fixed up here," Mr. Reilly said. "Then we'll go have a look at your horse."

ACTING AS IF SHE WERE doing nothing more than running to the store for a gallon of milk, Jessica waved her fingers at Rachel, then backed her car out of the garage, turned it around in a perfectly executed three-point turn and drove down the pretentiously long, winding driveway to Little Creek Road. And there, framed by the stone gates, she lost it.

She'd held herself together in front of Rachel, her friends and the various people she'd spoken to on the telephone, but her fragile self-control finally shattered. The shaking started deep within her, so she put the car in Park and rested her head on the steering wheel, taking deep breaths until the panic passed.

Think. To the right was the intersection of Pine Street and Little Creek. From there, it was a short block to the tree-lined street passing right by Lander Elementary. Jessica didn't think the bus went that direction. From the way Sam talked, it usually dropped off the kids who lived on Cottonwood Lane first.

So she'd try Cottonwood.

Just as soon as the shaking stopped.

"THAT OUGHTTA DO YA," Mr. Reilly said. "And I'll see what I can do about getting you a price on the Berkley's stuff.'' He scratched his head. "We don't get much call for that high-protein mix.''

"What are you feeding it to?'' Rex asked.

Max hefted the sack for Black Star. "I've got some exotics on the ranch, but a couple of years ago, one of the cows got into their feed. Seemed to like it, so I mixed some in with hers, and darned if she didn't have a prize-winning calf and become my best milker.''

"No kidding.'' Rex looked thoughtful, then started questioning Matt.

Matt eagerly told him and Mr. Reilly about his experiments with the high-protein feed originally meant for Sheba, the elderly tiger. He'd missed talking ranching with people who knew the life inside and out.

"Wonder if we should look into that. If there's one thing we need at Lost Springs, it's milk,'' Rex said.

Matt grinned. "Not many of the cows take to it, but those that do have good results.''

"Sounds like you're on to something.'' Mr. Reilly reached for a pad by the cash register and tore out a page. "Write down the mix and I'll suggest it to some of the ranchers around here.''

"You breeding the exotics?'' Rex asked as Matt wrote down the feed ratios.

"Not on purpose. I've got a little animal sanctuary going.'' He grimaced. "Didn't want them to end up on one of those fake safari places where people pretend to be big-game hunters.''

"I can see you doing something like that,'' Rex said. "You were always a soft touch. That's how you ended up with old Barnaby, isn't it?''

Before Matt could respond, he caught a movement through the feed store window. A young boy was climbing onto the truck's bumper. Once there, he inched his way onto the coupling, then found a precarious balance on the smooth wheel cover of the trailer. Hanging on to the edge of the metal lattice with one hand, he tried to pet Black Star with the other.

"Uh-oh, can't have that." Matt dropped the feedsack, then headed for the door, carefully opening it so the cowbell wouldn't clang and startle the boy.

"He's a beauty, isn't he?" he said when he was close enough to catch the boy in case he slipped off the wheel covering.

The boy nodded and withdrew his hand, which was what Matt hoped he'd do. "Is this your horse?"

"Yes."

"Does he perform flying feats of eq-equine artistry?"

"Beg pardon?"

"Do you make him leap through flaming hoops?"

"No…" Matt's gaze settled on the foggy images showing beneath the paint. "Oh—he's just borrowing another horse's trailer," he explained.

The boy looked relieved. "I was worried he might get burned."

"Not unless he backs into a campfire," Matt assured him.

"Does he bite?"

"He might. He's been cooped up there a long time and you're a stranger to him."

"I'm Samuel Fremont," the boy said in a rush. "I used to be Samuel Fremont the third, but my daddy and granddaddy died, so I'm Samuel Fremont all by myself now."

"Pleased to meet you, Samuel Fremont. I'm Matt Winston and this is Black Star."

The boy smiled, then said wistfully, "I sure would like to pet him."

"Well, let's see." Matt reached through the opening and rubbed Black Star's neck. The horse shifted, but didn't seem to be nervous or edgy. "Give me your hand."

Together he and Matt touched the horse. Matt felt a quiver, then realized it was Samuel. The boy was gazing at Black Star with unexpected intensity and longing. He didn't have the sure touch of someone used to being around animals, but if ever a boy wanted a horse, this one did.

The bell on the feed store door clanked. "Sam, is that you?"

"Hi, Mr. Reilly," Sam said without turning around. "I'm petting a horse."

"I see that." Mr. Reilly set the sack of feed Max had bought on the bench next to the store window. "What are you doing here this time of day?"

"Petting the horse."

Matt sent a questioning look toward Mr. Reilly and Rex, who'd joined him on the sidewalk.

"Does your mom know you're here?" Rex asked.

Sam kept running his hand over Black Star's neck.

"Sam?" Matt prodded.

"She doesn't care about me," Sam mumbled.

Those words were guaranteed to send a chill through a man with Matt's background, though his first impression of Sam hadn't been that he was a neglected boy, and Rex gave no indication that he was a Lost Springs resident.

"What makes you say that?" As Matt spoke, he studied the boy's clothes and scanned his arms and legs for signs of bruises. His shoes were a brand-name and worn, though fashionably so, not hand-me-down worn-out. His denim jeans fit and a little embroidered horse and rider were on his shirt. He looked better than okay to Matt.

"She's busy having a party with her *friends*," Sam grumbled. "She won't miss me."

Matt's jaw tightened. That kind of neglect was sometimes worse than the other. "Where do you live?"

Sam nodded eastward with his head.

"He lives in the Fremont house." Rex pointed.

Samuel Fremont. Matt hadn't made the connection. He automatically glanced toward the mansion set on a hill just high enough to overlook the rest of the town.

So Sam was a poor little rich kid with a mother who would rather spend time with her friends than her son. When Matt was at Lost Springs, people used to say the Fremonts had so much money it was a full-time job just spending it. All the boys, Matt included, secretly hoped they'd be discovered as the long-lost heir to the wealthy Fremont family.

He turned back to the blond-haired boy. And here was the actual Fremont heir. Poor kid. Matt had a good mind to take him home and give that selfish, overprivileged mother of his a lecture about responsibility.

"I saw you and your mom out at the ranch last weekend," Rex said. "I guess she's been busy helping with the auction."

Sam lifted his shoulder in an elaborately casual shrug and continued petting Black Star. If he kept it up, he was going to wear a bald spot on the horse.

"I believe I'm going to give your momma a call," Mr. Reilly said, and stepped back into his store.

"No!" Sam yelled after him.

Black Star flinched.

"She'll just get mad!"

"It's okay. I won't let her hurt you," Matt assured Sam.

"I don't want to go home!" Sam slid off the wheel fender. "I haven't finished making friends with Black Star yet."

A sport utility vehicle driving past on Cottonwood stopped so suddenly the tires squealed. The driver backed up, then turned the corner and came roaring toward them, pulling up beside the trailer. There weren't any parking spots, so she drove a little farther and double parked in front of the beauty parlor.

"*Ohhhh,* Sam." Rex leveled a look at the boy. "Your mother doesn't look too happy."

A blonde pushed open the door on the fancy car, not bothering to close it as she ran toward them. "Sam!"

Matt put a protective arm around the boy.

"Sam, I've been looking everywhere for you!" Heedless of Matt's arm, she pulled her son right out from under it and fell to her knees, clutching him to her. "Are you all right?"

Sam made a noise against her shoulder.

"Oh, Sam, I was so scared!" She swayed back and forth.

Even with the black picture he'd painted of her, Matt had to concede that this was no uncaring mother.

She had blond hair like her son's, though darker, and was wearing a long, loose flowered dress that pooled around her. Matt could see the muscles in her arms work as she tightly embraced her son.

There, being acted out right in front of him, was the dream of every boy at Lost Springs—a mother coming to take him home. The back of Matt's throat felt thick when he swallowed.

"Mom," Sam protested. "I'm *okay.*"

Still grasping his shoulders, she momentarily moved back. "I don't know whether to hug you or strangle you!"

"Looks like you're doing both," Matt said as a pair of blue eyes warily assessed him, then returned to Sam.

She loosened her grip on him, lightly running her hands over his arms and legs as she checked to make sure he was all right. "I've been looking everywhere for you." Satisfied that he wasn't hurt, she clutched him to her once more before rocking back on her heels.

Matt offered a hand to help her up and she unhesitatingly grasped it. *Strength,* he thought in the brief moment her hand was in his.

"Mom, I just wanted to see his horse."

"You should have checked with me first," she murmured with a questioning look at Rex.

"Jessica, this is Matt Winston. He's one of our bachelors for the auction."

"Oh, right." The reservation left her eyes and she offered her hand for a forthright shake. "Hello, Matt. Thanks for coming to support Lost Springs."

Once again, Matt had the impression of strength. Pretty blue-eyed strength in a flowered dress. A strength his own mother never had.

"Jessica's Fremont Construction has donated the extra bleachers for us."

"I assume the crew I sent out there this morning has finished cleaning up the site," she said to Rex, still keeping a protective hand on Sam's shoulder. "I'm not going to get the opportunity to inspect it myself ahead of time."

"They finished and it's looking good," Rex reassured her.

"Great." She glanced down at Sam. "We'd better

be getting back to the house. I have guests staying for the auction. Thanks for keeping an eye on him.'' She included Matt with a smile.

And that smile pretty much hit him right between the eyes. His feelings took a turn they had no business taking, not for a woman like Jessica Fremont, who was as deeply entrenched in Lightning Creek as he was at Winter Ranch.

He should say something instead of staring, but Rex was talking.

''Yeah, we were wondering if you knew where Sam was.''

''No, I did *not* know where he was,'' she said, glaring at her son. He hung his head, then looked up again.

''But, Mom, I *had* to see the horse.''

''Without telling me? I called everyone I could think of and I've been driving all around town hoping I'd find you.'' She drew him to her once more. ''Don't you ever take off like that again! You are to come home right after school lets out unless you tell me ahead of time.''

''It's only been a little while,'' he protested.

''Long enough for your grandmother to talk about calling Sheriff Hatcher!''

''Oh, come on!''

''You owe her an apology, Sam.''

Sam jerked away. ''I don't see what the big deal is! So I didn't come right inside after the bus dropped me off. Nobody else has to! You and Gramma keep treating me like I'm a baby!'' His lips quivered, and swallowing a sob, he ran across the street.

''Sam!'' Jessica called after him. ''You come back here right now!''

Of course he didn't. Matt could have told her that.

"What is the *matter* with him?" She started for her car.

"Is he running toward home?" Matt asked.

She turned to him, impatience coloring her voice. "Yes."

"Then just let him go."

"And lose him again?"

With his home visible from any place in town, Sam was unlikely to lose his way. "He'll make his own way home. He's lost face here. He can't come back after you dressed him down in front of us."

"Excuse me, but he's *my* son and you can bet I'm going to scold him after he scared me like that."

"He knows he's done wrong, but you didn't give him a chance to apologize before you embarrassed him."

There was no smile beaming Matt's way now. Jessica Fremont glared at him for one astonished, infuriated moment, then a mask settled over her features.

It was the darnedest thing, that mask. Her lips curved at the edges—Matt hated to call it a smile, because it was nothing like the one she'd directed at him before. "Thank you for your concern." She turned and walked toward her car, her steps deliberate, her back straight.

She was great.

"Mmm." Rex rubbed the back of his neck. "Criticizing Jessica's mothering might not have been the best way to impress her."

Matt watched her walk to her car, unable to stop himself. "She was wrong. And who said I was trying to impress her?"

Rex laughed. "I did."

CHAPTER FOUR

WHY WAS IT PEOPLE kept telling her how to raise her son?

Jessica could feel the rancher watching her as she walked to her car. He had an intense way of looking at a person that made her wonder if he could read her thoughts.

She couldn't believe he'd dared criticize her. It wasn't as though he had any kids of his own. She'd recognized him from the auction brochure as the rancher with the horse, and there wasn't anything in his bio about children, which meant he had no business telling her how to raise hers.

The fact that he might be right only made her madder.

The fact that he was good-looking and right made it intolerable.

It was ridiculous to get all worked up over some stranger's remarks. She was probably still emotional over the confrontation with Sam.

What had happened to her sweet little boy?

She'd just reached her car without tripping over anything when the door to Twyla's salon opened.

"Hello, Jessica."

Jessica's heart sank as she turned a smile toward Sugar Spinelli, a gossip with money—a lethal combination. Jessica liked her, but her mother-in-law didn't. It probably had something to do with the fact that the

Spinellis, due to oil being discovered on their ranch, were as well-off as the Fremonts, though more flamboyant.

Beside her was the silver-haired Mrs. Duckworth, retired third-grade teacher of nearly every native of Lightning Creek for the past thirty-five years. She'd taught Jessica's late husband, though she'd retired by the time Sam was in third grade last year.

"Having trouble with little Sammy?" Sugar blew on her newly painted nails.

"Everything's fine, Mrs. Spinelli."

She and Mrs. Duckworth glanced at the way Jessica's car blocked theirs. "It didn't appear that way to us, hon," said Mrs. Duckworth, indicating the glass front of the beauty parlor.

"Sam wanted to see the horse and I guess he was afraid I'd say no, so he decided to pay a visit without telling me." It was best to get the explanation over with.

The two women looked past her. "Yes, tell us about the horse and that fabulous man who's watching you as though you were the only woman on earth," Sugar said.

Jessica forced herself not to look.

"Oh, hon, if a man ever…" Mrs. Duckworth trailed off and cleared her throat. "Well, I'd at least look back, that's for darn sure."

Their words flustered Jessica, though she didn't dare show it. "He's Matt Winston, one of the bachelors in for the auction."

"Oh, good. He's here. Matthew!" trilled Mrs. Duckworth, waving her arm.

Jessica still didn't turn around.

"He was never in one of my classes, but I tutored him in reading. He was a bright boy, but he'd just missed so much school because of that mother of his dragging him all over the place.''

Don't ask. She didn't have to with Sugar Spinelli around.

''Drugs? Alcohol?''

Mrs. Duckworth gave Sugar a look. ''Men.''

''The poor boy,'' Sugar tut-tutted, shaking her head, her amethyst earrings swinging.

''They're all poor boys,'' Mrs. Duckworth said. ''But Lost Springs gives them a chance to make something of themselves, and all you have to do is read the brochure to see how successful they've become.''

''Are you bidding on anyone, Jessica?'' Sugar arched one eyebrow, still pink from the tweezing.

Jessica edged closer to her car. ''No, but I've got a couple of friends who are.''

''You should, hon.'' Mrs. Duckworth patted her on the arm. ''Samuel's been gone a long time and there's not a body in town who'd blink twice if you started stepping out again.''

''Don't believe her,'' Sugar said. ''They'd blink, but only because it's been such a long time.''

''Thank you. I, uh, need to get back to my houseguests.''

''You know, Sugar,'' Mrs. Duckworth was saying as Jessica got into her car. ''There are just too many single mothers in this town.''

''Am I not doing my part?'' Sugar protested.

''I guess you are. Now, come here and let me introduce you to Matthew.''

Single mother. On the drive home, Jessica thought about what they'd said. She'd never thought of herself as a single mother before, but she supposed that's what she was. *Single mother* brought to mind a woman who struggled alone and with too little money. Jessica had always had Rachel around to help—and the ghosts of her husband and his father. She'd never had financial worries, but now she saw that she'd paid for this security by changing herself.

She'd been locked into a way of life and hadn't known it because she'd never tried to get out the door. But between Sam's horse and cowboy obsession and Rachel's attitude toward Jessica's friends, she now found herself disagreeing and arguing with her mother-in-law. To her surprise, Rachel simply stated how things would be and assumed Jessica would fall into line. And why not? Hadn't she always?

It had been easier for Jessica to go along with Rachel's ideas of how she should live and Sam should be raised. That way she didn't have to think, to make decisions or expose herself emotionally.

She couldn't believe the woman she'd become. Sam barely knew Jessica's own parents. Granted, they still traveled as much as ever, but on their few visits here, Rachel had been no more than coldly polite. And Jessica had made no effort to visit them on her own.

She turned into the Fremont private driveway and wondered how she'd come to be in the state she was in—and how she was going to convince Rachel that she didn't intend to be the passive daughter-in-law anymore.

THANKFULLY, breakfast the next morning was very casual. After the strain of trying to pretend that everything was just peachy keen after Sam arrived home last night, Jessica was exhausted.

She'd made a big pot of coffee and set out bagels, muffins and fresh fruit and let Tara and Liz fend for themselves. They were back upstairs getting ready for the auction and Jessica had just poured herself a second cup of coffee when Sam came in looking for breakfast.

"Bakery muffins!" He grabbed a blueberry one while Jessica poured him a glass of milk. Yesterday's sulking appeared to be past, for which Jessica was grateful.

She was even more grateful that the brochure for Camp Whispering Pines had arrived in yesterday's mail. She'd looked it over last night and was encouraged by what she'd seen. Except for the horses, there wasn't anything Rachel should object to.

"Guess what?" Jessica said. "The camp brochure came yesterday."

Sam's eyes widened. "Why didn't you tell me?"

"You were sulking in your room."

"Oh. Yeah." He looked cowed for about half a second. "Let me see!"

"It's on the phone table."

Sam scrambled from his seat and raced across the kitchen. "Can I go? Can I?"

"It looks good, but I need to do a little more checking, and you've got to realize that it's already June. They might be full," she cautioned.

Sam was pawing through the papers, making a mess in the process. "I can't find it."

"It should be right on top." Carrying her coffee with her, Jessica went to help him look. It wasn't there.

"I imagine you're looking for this." They hadn't heard Rachel come into the kitchen. She carefully set the camp brochure on the breakfast table.

Something about the way she did so sent a flicker of apprehension through Jessica.

"Hey!" Sam ran back over to the table. "Let me see!"

One look at Rachel's tight face and Jessica knew she was still facing an uphill battle to convince her mother-in-law to let Sam go. Well, Jessica wasn't thrilled about Sam's cowboy and horse obsession, either, but the brochure stressed that campers would be responsible for chores and caring for their assigned horse. Jessica hoped that a couple of weeks of the realities of a cowboy's life would be enough for Sam. By denying him the opportunity to see what being a cowboy was like, they were only letting him glamorize the life.

"The pictures make the camp seem—" she began.

"Sam," Rachel interrupted her.

He looked up, his smile fading at the tone in his grandmother's voice.

"Yesterday, you didn't come home after the bus let you off. We had no idea where you were."

"I wanted to see the horse," Sam said in a small voice.

"And so you did. But such actions have consequences."

Jessica felt it was time to intervene. "I think that Sam knows he frightened us yesterday and won't make that mistake in the future."

She looked at Sam, who immediately shook his head. "No, I won't."

Rachel frowned. "I don't share your conviction that Sam has learned from his behavior, so to help him remember, I called Camp Whispering Pines."

Jessica got a sick feeling in her stomach.

"They had three openings left. I purchased them and have donated them to the Ladies Auxiliary to be awarded to three needy children. Whispering Pines is now full for the summer.'' Her eyes were bright.

"Rachel," Jessica whispered an instant before a howl erupted from Sam.

"Full? You mean I can't go?"

"We do not reward misbehavior in this house."

"No!"

Rachel leveled a look at him. "And furthermore, there will be no more talk of horses, young man."

He turned to Jessica. "Mom?" His voice broke.

Jessica stared at her mother-in-law, appalled that Rachel had put her in this position. "Sam, I'll think of something. I don't know what just now, but you'll get to go to a camp. I promise."

"Jessica, it isn't appropriate—"

"Would you leave us, please?"

Rachel hesitated. "I wouldn't have had to take action myself if I could have depended upon you to do so."

Jessica put her hands on Sam's shoulders. He was trying not to cry, but tears had already spilled onto his cheeks. "Oh, don't worry. I'm going to take action."

Without another word, Rachel left the room.

"I knew she wouldn't let me go," Sam said with a sniff. He'd stopped crying, but the leaden sound to his voice was worse.

"Sam, I told you I'd think of something. Just give me a few minutes."

"Mom." The look he gave her was resigned. "Get real."

Her own son didn't believe she could stand up to Rachel. That shook Jessica more than anything else. It hurt, too. But why should he think differently? He'd never seen his mother in action before.

Okay, she'd promised Sam she'd make up for what

Rachel had done, so she'd have to think of something. Fast.

An image of a man's arm protectively draped around her son's shoulder came to mind. Matt Winston's arm.

Yesterday, she'd been so relieved to find Sam that she hadn't paid much attention to what he'd been doing, but in replaying that moment, she remembered pulling Sam to her. There'd been a brief resistance, and she realized that Matt was making sure Sam would be okay with her before releasing him.

There hadn't been anything threatening in the rancher's stance, but Jessica had no doubt that if she'd been found lacking in those dark, intense eyes, Sam would still be under his protection.

If Sam was ever going to ride a horse, then that was the man Jessica wanted teaching him.

And it just so happened that he was up for auction in a few hours.

There were times, though not so many in recent years, when Jessica impulsively acted on pure instinct. It had been that way when she'd decided to spend the rest of her life with Sam's father, and it was that way now.

"Sam, run, get dressed. I'm taking you to the auction with us."

THEY PARKED in the makeshift lot next to the soccer field. Jessica took Sam's hand and headed purposefully toward the show arena where the auction would be held.

"Here we are, trolling for men. Just like old times, right, Jessica?" Liz eyed the milling crowd around the barbecue.

"I plan to buy a horse," Jessica murmured under her breath. "The man just happens to be attached."

"That's what they all say," Liz scoffed good-naturedly. "Now, who goes home with me tonight?"

"Shh. The kid's with us." Tara jerked her head toward Sam, who was oblivious to everything but the horse stables they were walking past.

"I remember."

Liz hadn't been enthusiastic about Jessica bringing Sam with them to the auction, but she didn't care.

"Jessica, I haven't seen you so single-minded in years." Liz raised an eyebrow. "Welcome back."

"It's good to be back," she said, and meant it.

"Yeah, and slow down," Tara complained. "These boots are killing my feet. The auction won't start until after the barbecue, right?"

"Like you have any room to eat in those jeans," her sister said.

"Jealous?"

Liz tossed her head. "Comfortable."

"Mom, there's Black Star!" Sam pointed toward the stables and pulled Jessica's hand.

Jessica saw the horse, but she also saw the man grooming him. At first she admired the contrast his white shirt made against the animal, then she admired the form beneath the fitted shirt. She'd been too relieved at finding Sam, then angry at being criticized to notice much about Matt Winston yesterday.

He had a nice set of shoulders. Just right for giving boys piggyback rides. Just right for...well, she'd stick with the piggyback image for now.

"Let's go see him!" Sam urged.

Glad to get away from the sisters' bickering and anxious to take another look at the man she wanted to spend time with her son, Jessica allowed Sam to pull her along. "Kids," she said by way of explanation.

Tara and Liz waved her away. "We're going to check out the merchandise." Laughing, they strutted toward the arena.

YOU COULDN'T SELL A HORSE without showing him to people, and Matt wanted Black Star looking his considerable best, which meant putting this goop the circus people used on his mane and tail. It sure did make horse hair shine, even without added glitter, but he hoped he didn't have to explain what he was doing to anybody.

"Mr. Winston!"

Matt wasn't called Mr. Winston all that often and it felt strange, especially here at Lost Springs. He knew it was the Fremont boy even before he looked up.

"Hey, Sam." *Hey, Sam's mother.* Matt nodded to her, not sure of her mood after yesterday.

Her smile showed she was making an effort, but it was a little tight around the mouth. "Hello. Sam wanted to visit your horse." She swallowed.

"His name's Black Star. Hi, Black Star." Sam reached out.

"Hang on." Matt intercepted his hand. "Let him see you first." Gently he led the boy to Black Star's nose.

"Hi, Black Star! Remember me?"

Black Star wasn't any too happy about being uprooted and had been testy this morning with Matt. He wasn't being much friendlier to Sam.

Fortunately, Lita, Matt's cook, had packed some of her rocklike gingersnaps with his lunch for the drive here. Horses and various other animals loved Lita's gingersnaps. The local dentist did, too.

"Here. Try feeding one of these to him." Matt stepped to the stall door, where he'd draped a tooled leather vest that Frank had insisted he wear during the auction. Of course Frank had meant *instead* of a shirt, but that wasn't Matt's style. Reaching into a pocket, he pulled out a plastic bag and gave Sam a cookie piece. "Flatten your hand."

Sam did. Black Star's nose twitched and he deigned to take the cookie.

"It tickles!" Sam laughed and wiped his hands on his shorts.

Matt grinned and glanced at Jessica.

Her smile was wide, but her eyes were bright and she looked like she was about to cry.

What's all that about? Matt was curious, but wasn't going to embarrass her by asking.

"Mom, did you see?"

Nodding and smiling, she tucked her hair behind her ear and wrapped her arms in front of her, as if she had to force herself to keep from grabbing Sam away from the horse.

"Sam, if I remember from my days here, that last stall has some steps in it. If you drag those over here, I'll let you help curry."

"Okay!" Sam took off.

"Other way," Matt directed him, and Sam reversed directions so fast Matt chuckled.

"I don't think he even knows what currying is," Jessica said. Now that Sam wasn't next to the horse, she'd relaxed somewhat.

"You don't mind, do you?"

"No. You're very kind. Very patient."

But she still seemed stiff, which meant she was probably mad about him interfering yesterday.

Matt wanted to clear the air. "Listen. I'd like to apologize for yesterday."

She looked genuinely puzzled. "What for?"

"Sticking my nose in your business."

"With Sam?"

"Yeah."

"Oh, no! In fact, you were right, and as you see, he made it home okay." She watched Sam drag the steps across the dirt.

Matt watched her and fiddled with the currycomb. She didn't act like one of the wealthy Fremonts—or the way he always thought a Fremont would act if he'd run across one in town.

But she was one. Yeah, she was wearing jeans and a denim shirt, but there was something about the way she wore them. They fit just so, and the black leather belt with the heavy silver buckle she wore was obviously well made. When she tucked her blond hair behind her ear, he saw little silver hoop earrings.

He'd seen other women wearing similar outfits, but Jessica looked different. Classy.

Out of reach.

Still, he was glad she wasn't the type to carry a grudge. Even though he'd go back to his ranch and never see her again, knowing that they'd parted on less-than-genial terms would have eaten at him. He'd be a fool to feel that way, but there it was.

"Are these okay, Mr. Winston?" A red-faced Sam indicated the old wooden steps that dozens of boys had stood on to perform chores in the stables.

"Call me Matt, Sam. Those are the ones. Pull them right around here."

He positioned the boy and stood behind him, showing him how to hold the currycomb and brush Black Star.

"It's sticky." Sam made a face.

"That's the dressing," Matt said in a low voice. "Just comb it on through."

The whole time he was conscious that Jessica watched them. He hadn't quite figured her out yet. But he sure would like to.

"HEY, THERE YOU ARE, MATT." Carrying a clipboard, Rex Trowbridge approached them. "Hi, Jessica, Sam. Say, Matt, you planning to mingle anytime soon? You need to set a few hearts to fluttering so the bids will run up."

Matt gave him a look that made Jessica laugh. At the sound, both men glanced at her. She saw a flicker of masculine interest in Rex's eyes.

She saw considerably more than a flicker in Matt's. It was a steady beam that told her he found her attractive right at that moment and didn't mind her knowing.

What an unexpected lift. How long had it been since a man had looked at her that way?

How long had it been since she'd *wanted* a man to look at her that way?

Flattered and a little nonplussed, she said, "Seems to be a good turnout."

"Yeah," Rex said. "We've even got a couple of news vans out here. Have you been interviewed yet?" he asked Matt.

"No."

"Now don't be shy." Rex was grinning.

"You're pushing it, Rex."

"And lovin' every minute."

"How's that, Matt?" Sam interrupted them. While they'd been talking, he'd been industriously combing through Black Star's mane.

"Looking good, Sam." Matt covered the boy's hand with his and edged the comb over to a spot he'd missed.

Matt had strong, sure hands with a gentle touch. Sam

smiled up at him with the pure trust of a child, and Jessica's breath caught.

It might be a very expensive afternoon, because she was going to pay any amount of money to bring that expression to her son's face again. This was a man she could trust, a man who made her son happy.

And he made you happy for a minute, too, didn't he?

Matt gave his horse a pat. "Okay, Sam. Looks like we're done."

Sam looked disappointed, but he didn't argue.

"Go ahead and put the stairs away," Matt directed.

Sam instantly hopped off the wooden steps and began dragging them back to the stall. He didn't respond so quickly when Jessica asked him to do his chores around the house.

"You know, you ought to ride your horse in the show ring during the bidding," Rex suggested. "He was in the brochure picture and all." Then he added with a chuckle, "Maybe we could auction him off, too."

"I'll ride him in the ring, but I wouldn't want folks to think they were kicking in money for Lost Springs when they were just buying my horse," Matt said with a significant look at Rex.

Buying his horse?

Rex grinned. "Can't blame me for trying. We're going to start in about half an hour. If we can get the loudspeaker system to work, there'll be an announcement. All us fine bachelors will be sitting by the podium." Touching the brim of his hat he strode off.

Matt was murmuring to Black Star as he curried the mane between his ears.

"Are you selling your horse?" Jessica asked. If he was, then that would defeat the purpose of bidding on him at the auction.

Matt's jaw tightened, and he nodded. "That's why I brought him with me from Texas."

"You didn't tell Sam, did you?"

"No. I wouldn't do that." He glanced at her, then turned his attention back to the horse. "Sam's taken a shine to him, though."

"Sam's 'taken a shine' to horses in general."

"If you're in the market for a horse, you could do a lot worse than Black Star. I've raised him since he was a colt and he's a fine animal."

Jessica heard him swallow and stared at him. "You love that horse, don't you?"

Matt gave a quick nod, but said determinedly, "He's just a horse. Now, I have to admit he might be too much horse for young Sam right now, but not after he's had experience."

"Why are you selling him when you don't want to?"

Matt was silent for so long, Jessica didn't think he would answer her. "Money." He exhaled. "Bad drought in Texas last year meant we had to buy feed for cattle in the summer instead of letting them graze. It appears this summer won't be much better."

"I'm sorry." The words came automatically, but Jessica realized she meant them.

He looked down at her. "Thanks." He didn't look away, but held her gaze.

Jessica didn't look away, either.

She didn't know how long they stood in the stable yard, just staring at each other, because oddly, she didn't feel the slightest bit awkward. It was probably only a few seconds, but in those seconds Jessica felt herself emotionally connecting with someone other than her immediate family for the first time since her husband had died.

She shouldn't be feeling anything for this rancher— but it was nice to know she could.

CHAPTER FIVE

SHOULD SHE TELL MATT she was going to bid on him? Find out what kind of date he'd planned? Not that it mattered. All she wanted was for him to spend some time with Sam.

A lot of time.

Sam came running back. "Now what do we do, Matt?"

"Now we go eat lunch," Jessica said.

"I want to stay here with Matt," Sam announced. "I could help him."

Jessica was gearing up for another public parent-child power struggle when Matt spoke.

"Wish you could, Sam, but Black Star and I've got to meet with a couple of fellas in a few minutes. Maybe you can come see me after the auction."

Come see me after the auction. The words prompted an idea. Why not *really* come see him—at his ranch? Sam was missing out on the horse camp, so why couldn't they go to Matt's ranch instead? It would be a more authentic experience than camp, anyway.

She wasn't ready to buy a horse—no telling what Rachel would do—but taking Sam to the ranch would let him see what it was like to be a cowboy.

Naturally Jessica would go with him. It would also give them some much-needed time away from Rachel and make it clear to her son that she, Jessica, was the one in charge, not his grandmother.

Would Matt agree?

Jessica didn't plan to give him a choice. If she made the winning bid, she got to choose the date, right?

Would a couple of weeks on a ranch count as a date?

She'd convince him. After all, he needed money. She had money. They'd work something out.

"You hungry, Sam?" she asked after she'd finally pried him away from Matt.

"Man, am I!"

Jessica handed him a few dollars for meal tickets and got in the line for brisket, sausage and chicken.

She and Sam ate barbecue, then went in search of Liz and Tara. They found them reminiscing about their school days with a harried-looking Lindsay.

Tara saw her first. "Hey, Jessica! We saved you a seat in the front row."

Everyone knew Rachel Fremont disapproved of the auction and Jessica felt about a million pairs of interested eyes watching her take her seat. She could hear whispers buzzing through the arena. They probably couldn't wait to see how she could behave with Fremont-like decorum while shouting out bids for a man.

Tara had meant it when she said "a" seat, so Jessica tried to get Sam to sit on her lap.

"Mom…" he protested.

Jessica made Tara and Liz squeeze over so Sam could share her seat on the risers. He was getting big. Or there was the possibility that *she* was getting big, which didn't bear thinking about.

A few of the bachelors had taken their places on folding chairs around the auctioneer's podium. Feminine murmurs accompanied by the flutter of brochure pages eddied around them.

"Oh, my, *my,* my, my." Liz stared admiringly as a couple of the guys grew tired of sitting and jumped up and started posing for the women.

"Lindsay promised it wasn't going to be like that," Jessica murmured, mindful of her son taking all this in.

"Jessica, I realize this is serious business, but you are just *too* serious." Tara poked her shoulder. "Lighten up. You're supposed to be having fun!"

One of the men undid two buttons on his shirt.

"Yeah!" Tara put two fingers in her mouth and let out a piercing whistle.

So much for Fremont decorum.

"Cool!" Sam leaned forward. "Can you teach me to do that?"

When Tara nodded, he switched places with Jessica, and for the next several minutes, Tara whistled and Sam spluttered.

Tara's whistles loosened up the women, not that they needed much encouragement.

"We want men!" The chant started somewhere— Jessica suspected with Liz—and was quickly picked up.

Moments later, the auctioneer strode to the podium and cheers erupted.

Matt still hadn't taken his place. Had he changed his mind? There were a couple of other cowboy types that Jessica could bid on, but Sam liked Matt and his horse.

She liked Matt…and his horse.

What if he was selling Black Star right now? That would be disastrous. Nearly convincing herself that she was only concerned on Sam's behalf, Jessica twisted around, trying to see outside the show arena as the auctioneer picked up the microphone.

"Ladies and gentlemen, I have been asked to announce that this is the last chance to buy a raffle ticket for the beautiful Log Cabin quilt donated by the Converse County Quilt Quorum."

There wasn't a mad dash for the exit, even if it was a beautiful quilt.

"All right then," the auctioneer continued. "Before we get started, Ms. Lindsay Duncan has a few words she'd like to say to you."

Jessica clapped politely as a smiling Lindsay stood at the podium and thanked everyone for coming and encouraged them to bid high. "And a special thank you to Fremont Construction for donating the extra bleachers."

"Aw-right, Jessie!" Tara whistled and Sam spit a bunch.

Jessica smiled, and wondered how soon her mother-in-law would get a report of the afternoon's activities.

The auctioneer returned, gave them the rules for the afternoon and instructions for paying. "So ladies, put your hands together for our first bachelor, Dr. Robert Carter."

"So *that's* Lauren's Rob," Liz said. "Tara, he deserves a whistle."

Tara and her protégé obliged.

"Now where did I put my checkbook?" Liz had already raised her hand for the opening bid.

"Liz, I can't believe you're bidding on him!" Tara laughed. "What are you going to do if you actually win him?"

"Take pictures and send them to Lauren."

But Liz had severe competition. The bids went higher and higher. Each time she raised her arm, there was an immediate response from another bidder. She frowned. "Who *is* that?"

Jessica leaned forward and looked down the row. "Sugar Spinelli." How very interesting.

"How high can she go?"

"As high as she wants."

Sugar raised the bid.

"And it looks like she wants Rob," Jessica said.

"Oh, well, then. Let her have him. I only wanted to tweak Lauren. I had no intention of getting into *serious* money. For serious money, I'll buy someone available."

Liz shook her head at the auctioneer when he looked at her questioningly.

A few minutes later, Sugar Spinelli had bought the first bachelor amid thunderous applause and whistling.

"Ow!" Sam took his fingers out of his mouth. "I popped my ear."

"You're blowing too hard," Tara said.

Sam rubbed his ear. "Mom, what's going on, anyway?"

Jessica explained the general gist of a bachelor auction in terms designed to avoid psychologically scarring a nine-year-old boy.

At that moment, Matt Winston finally joined the others on stage. He tied Black Star's reins to a support pole and sat in one of the folding chairs.

"Hey, there's Matt!" Sam tried whistling to get his attention, but got frustrated and waved instead.

"And do we have a bid from...?"

Jessica shook her head and captured Sam's hands. "No waving."

"Who's going to buy Matt?"

Jessica made a promise she hoped she would be able to keep. "We are."

After that, the auction seemed to take forever. There were serious bidders and serious bids. The women paid amounts high enough to make even Jessica blink.

Liz and Tara tried to draw her into financing the bidding wars with a group bid, but Jessica shook her head.

This was ridiculous. Why take a chance? She should just go make a donation and ask for Matt. An anonymous donor had already done that with another bachelor. Lindsay was a friend. She'd tell her how much it was.

But the moment when she could have done such a thing was past.

The auctioneer took a drink of water. "Ladies, here's another chance for the date of your dreams. Matt Winston."

BEING NEARLY LAST was the pits. By now, all these women were probably broke.

Matt had been late to the auction because he'd had a few nibbles about Black Star, which should have encouraged him, but ended up making him feel sorry for himself. And that made him mad because he didn't have any right feeling sorry for himself. So he had to sell his horse. Big deal. He'd been a lot worse off in his life.

And this getting a sponsor business…he just didn't have the guts to go out and ask for money the way Rex did. No, that was going to take some thinking. Maybe whoever bought the date with him would put him in touch with organizations who were into that sort of thing.

As his turn grew closer, he tried remembering everything Frank had told him. He picked out a woman in the bleachers and gazed soulfully at her, but she avoided his eyes and eventually grabbed the hand of the woman sitting next to her and left.

He should have mingled. He was going to regret not mingling. He was going to ride Black Star around in circles and nobody was going to give a plug nickel for him.

He kept stealing glances at Jessica and Sam. As far as he could tell, she hadn't bid on anyone, which pleased him, though it shouldn't.

As soon as the winning bid was placed on the man who'd been sitting next to him, Matt untied Black Star.

The auctioneer paused and took a drink of water. Matt swallowed, his mouth suddenly dry. Water would be really great right now. Then he heard his name.

He swung into the saddle and rode Black Star right up onto the stage.

He might have been imagining it, but to him, the applause was louder than it had been for a while.

Black Star had learned a few tricks and Matt set out to show him off. He pulled the reins tight, which was the signal for the horse to arch his neck and paw the ground.

The audience "oohed" and the applause swelled.

"Our next bachelor, Matt Winston, is the owner of Winter Ranch in the beautiful Texas Hill Country. Matt's riding his horse, Black Star!"

Another signal and Black Star bowed.

"He's looking for a strong woman who'll stick with him through thick and thin," the auctioneer said. "So, ladies, who'll give me our minimum bid?"

Matt didn't even have time to say a quick prayer before, incredibly, there were two bids—one of which sounded like it came from a young boy.

He couldn't help it. He looked toward Jessica and Sam. Sam was waving his hand in the air and Jessica supported his arm so the auctioneer would know it was a genuine bid.

She wasn't looking at him, but he looked at her. Her face was pale, except for a little bit of color on her cheekbones.

She was being polite, that was it. Jessica Fremont seriously bidding on Matt Winston? Come on.

And yet he couldn't stop himself from imagining taking Jessica on the picnic he'd planned. They'd ride and he'd show her all the places he remembered from his years here, including the massive tree that had bent down and formed a leafy cave. When he'd been young, he and the other boys had pretended it was a fort, but the adult Matt knew it would make a perfect picnic spot.

He'd brought a huge soft quilt with him and suddenly found himself looking forward to an event he'd previously dreaded—but only if Jessica made the winning bid.

Two more bids rang out and she and Sam topped them, ensuring that Matt wouldn't be sold for the least amount of money.

Pleased, he made Black Star bow in their direction again.

He should be riding him instead of just sitting, anyway. Holding the reins tightly again, he gently nudged Black Star, who raised his tail and walked off the stage to high step his way around the ring.

Sam cheered and clapped with the rest of the crowd.

"Thirty-five hundred," the auctioneer cried, and Matt nearly fell off his horse.

Yeah, some of the amounts paid for the men had been

much higher, but he didn't think there was such a thing as a thirty-five-hundred-dollar picnic.

JESSICA'S ARM was getting tired, and so was her face. Keeping the Fremont mask in place at all times was a harder habit to break than she'd thought it would be.

"Look!" Sam pointed and clapped as Matt made his horse prance around the ring.

Jessica was afraid to look. She'd already looked once and hadn't been prepared for the striking picture the man and his horse made.

Matt wore black jeans and had added a black leather vest over his blinding white shirt. Together with the gleaming black horse, he looked...good. Really good. Jessica wasn't prepared for more intense descriptions just now. "Four thousand!" The bid sounded right in her ear.

Liz.

Jessica raised her hand.

"Forty-five hundred?" the auctioneer asked.

Jessica nodded.

"Who'll give—and we have five thousand."

A group of women had huddled together on the bleachers across from them. "Six!" one of them shouted triumphantly.

Jessica waved again.

Someone else did, too.

"Oh, forever more. Seven!" Liz again.

"Hey, Liz..." Tara had stopped whistling back at five thousand. "What are you doing?"

"Bidding."

"And we have seven thousand from the pretty lady in the front," cried the auctioneer.

"Is that you, Mom?"

"It will be." Jessica nudged him. "Wave your arm, Sam."

"Mr. Auction Man!" Sam jumped up and down to get his attention.

"And the bid would be for...?"

Jessica held up both hands, her fingers splayed.

"We have ten thou-ou-ou-sand dollars!"

Applause broke out.

"Ten-five," Liz called out. "I want that cowboy. I find myself suddenly drawn to all that power between his—"

"Hush!" Tara muzzled her sister.

Jessica raised the bid to eleven. It was much easier to bid with the zeros removed in her mind.

"Eleven-five," Liz bid promptly.

"Hey, Liz. Cut it out," Tara said.

"Why?"

"Jessica is bidding against you."

"So?" Liz looked determined.

Jessica nodded to Sam, who, in his excitement, had climbed onto the bleachers next to her. He jumped and waved, making them all shake.

Jessica felt Tara look at her. She turned and smiled blandly.

Tara stared at her, then poked Liz. "Jessica, who hasn't shown an interest in any man since her husband died, is prepared to fork over at least twelve *thousand* dollars for this one. Let her have him."

Liz licked her lips. "She's not ready for a man like that yet." She made a kissing motion and signaled the auctioneer. "Thirteen's always been my lucky number, anyway."

Now that Jessica thought about it, had she and Liz ever really been close? "Go, Sam," she said.

The catcalls had stopped and so had most of the talking. An unnatural hush descended over the crowd as people waited for the outcome.

"I don't know what she thinks she's doing," Tara said to Jessica in a low voice.

"Making it very difficult for me to explain this to my mother-in-law, that's what."

Sam overheard them. "How much money can we spend?" His voice carried.

Jessica raised hers. "As much as we need to, sweetie. Mommy's been saving her allowance."

Liz leaned forward. "Now, Jessica, honey, let's not lose our friendship over this."

"I agree. Stop bidding against me."

"No." She raised her hand but Tara yanked it down.

"We have fourteen thousand going once…"

"Fif—" Tara held her hand over Liz's mouth.

"Do I hear fifteen?" The auctioneer clearly didn't know what to do.

Tara managed to keep her hand over her sister's mouth and climbed onto her lap.

"…going twice…"

"Will you just call it sold already!" she yelled.

"Sold to Jessica Fremont for fourteen thousand dollars!"

"Yea! I'm going to tell Matt." Sam jumped off the bleachers and headed toward Matt, who'd swung off the horse. "Hey, Matt, we bought you!" Jessica heard him yell.

She'd done it. Now what?

"Oh, get off me," grumbled Liz to her sister. "I'm tuned in now." She straightened her blouse then blew Matt a kiss. "Bye-bye, cowboy." Sighing, she faced

Jessica. "Why didn't you tell me you were buying him for the kid?"

Jessica was still miffed with her. Standing on shaky legs, she smiled. "Because only the horse was for Sam."

MATT WAS NUMB. She'd just bid...just bid... He couldn't even wrap his mind around a figure that big.

And for him. Why did she do it?

When a woman made a gesture like that, charity or not, it meant something. Matt had no idea what. He sure hoped she'd tell him. There were bound to be certain expectations on her part, and he would do his best to live up to them, whatever they were.

Talk about pressure.

Matt nodded to Sam, who was jumping all around, caught up in the excitement, and led him out of the auction area.

"Where's your mama?" he asked.

"With her friends. I told her I was going to find you. Watch what I can do. Tara was teaching me to whistle." He put two fingers in his mouth and blew.

Nothing much but air and spit came out.

Matt laughed. "Either she's not much of a teacher, or you're going to have to work on that."

"She whistles real good. Didn't you hear her?"

To tell the truth, and he didn't plan to, Matt had been so shocked at seeing Jessica bidding for him, he hadn't heard much of anything. He'd forgotten all Frank's advice about soulful looks and had stared blindly into the crowd.

Was this what Frank and the others felt during their performances? If so, Matt was perfectly happy staying in the background.

And he'd once wanted to be a rodeo champion.

Well, now what? He sure could use some of that ice-cold lemonade.

People, mostly women, were standing around watching. Jessica wasn't one of them. She might be in the crowd by the bleachers, but he couldn't tell.

"Come on, Sam. Let's take Black Star for a little walk." He bent and laced his fingers together.

"You mean...you mean I can *ride* him?"

"Sure. Put your foot here, and when I give you a boost, grab the saddle horn and pull yourself up."

Sam put a sneaker-clad foot in his hands and Matt helped him into the saddle. When he straightened, Sam was white-knuckling the saddle horn as Black Star side-stepped.

"First time on a horse?" Matt asked.

Sam gave a jerky nod. "He's big."

"That he is." Matt gathered the reins and slowly walked Black Star farther away from the arena.

Sam's eyes were round and he wasn't smiling much. Matt couldn't tell whether he was happy about being on Black Star or not.

"You're not going to let go of the reins, are you?"

Matt smiled up at him. "Nope."

"Good." He relaxed a little, but still clutched the saddle horn.

Continuing to walk slowly, Matt headed toward the stables. He figured Jessica would eventually find them. "You know, right around here is where I first rode a horse."

"Here, at Lost Springs?"

Matt nodded.

"You mean you lived here?"

"Yeah."

Sam thought about that for a moment. "Was it fun?"

Fun. He'd never thought of Lost Springs as a fun place. But... "I had some good times. I missed my mother, so I wasn't too happy to be here. But if I couldn't be with her, Lost Springs was a pretty good place."

"Why couldn't you live with your mother?"

The memory of the last time he saw his mother was as clear as the day she left. They'd been living in Amarillo only a few weeks, not long enough for the landlord to evict them yet. He'd come home from school and she'd been all excited—and sober for once. Buddy, a trucker she'd been dating, was going to take her with him on a run from Amarillo to Kansas City. She'd promised she'd be back in a few days. She'd left Matt milk, three boxes of his favorite cereal and five cans of chicken noodle soup.

Even today he couldn't stomach sugary cereal or canned chicken noodle soup.

But Sam didn't need to know about such things, so Matt said only, "She couldn't take care of me and there was a judge who thought I'd be better off here for a while."

And he had been. But it had taken a long time for him to realize it.

"How long did you live here?"

"Seven years."

"Wow."

Footsteps crunched behind them. Matt looked over his shoulder and saw Jessica hurrying toward them. He stopped walking until she caught up.

"Mom, look at me!" Sam cried before they could say anything to each other.

"I see you!" Her smile was strained, or maybe that was Matt's imagination. "Do you like it up there?"

Sam nodded.

"Are you going to the stables?" she asked Matt.

"Yeah. Thought I'd get Black Star away from the crowd."

"Good idea. I don't want to get caught by another reporter. He had a photographer with him, and they wanted a picture of us together." She made a face.

Matt didn't particularly care if he had his picture taken or not, but Jessica seemed upset by the idea.

He continued toward the stables and she fell into step with him.

"About the auction...I don't know what to say," Matt admitted. "Thanks doesn't seem right for the amount of money you just spent. I know it means the world to Lindsay."

"The money's not important," Jessica said, brushing her hair back from her face.

To Matt, the money was always important. In that one careless comment, Jessica Fremont turned a spotlight on the gulf between them, and no picnic was going to bridge it.

"They didn't tell us what we were supposed to do after the auction was over," he said. "So I'm winging it here." He glanced down at her. "I don't know if I'll be able to give you the date of your dreams, but I intend to do my best."

"Yes, well, about that..." She cleared her throat.

Matt could swear she was nervous.

"Sam, some of the boys are over at the playground. Why don't you go over there while I talk with Matt?"

Sam's face turned mutinous. "I want to ride Black Star."

"I'm going to take the saddle off him when we get to the stables anyway," Matt said. "If your mom says it's okay, you can stay on until then." It was only a couple hundred more feet.

Jessica obviously knew it wasn't a battle worth fighting and nodded her agreement.

In a few minutes, they'd reached Black Star's stall and Matt had helped Sam slide down. He lingered until Matt hooked a thumb toward the playground. "Scoot."

Though he obviously didn't want to, Sam scooted.

They watched until he was out of earshot.

"I guess you want to—"

"I suppose you're wondering why—"

They both spoke at the same time, then laughed. The tension broke.

"I realize you were donating to charity and all, but good grief, woman," Matt said.

"Yeah." Jessica looked a little shell-shocked herself. "Listen, you haven't sold your horse yet, have you?"

Matt uncinched Black Star. "I'm about to, I think."

"Please don't. At least not until Sam has the opportunity to learn to ride him."

Matt glanced at her. "You could buy him yourself and then Sam could ride him all he wanted."

"I can't."

"Why not? You just dropped a chunk of change at the auction."

"It's complicated." She ran both hands through her hair. He liked the way it swung back into place and caught the late afternoon sunlight.

Matt slid the saddle off Black Star. "I'm listening."

"You need to know that Sam's father was killed on a horse."

That caught him off guard. No wonder they were

both antsy around Black Star. "I'm sorry," he said, and propped the saddle across the stall railing. "What happened?"

"He was posing for pictures next to a fence and a photographer's flash startled the horse. Samuel fell off and hit his head. Broke his neck. His father saw the whole thing and had a heart attack. Three days later, he was dead, too."

It was a story worn smooth by repeated telling. She'd distilled it down to bare, unemotional facts, the way the boys at Lost Springs all learned to tell their various stories.

No wonder she hadn't wanted to have her picture taken with a horse. "I'm sorry, Jessica," he repeated. "It must have been awful for you."

"Yes, it was." She drew a deep breath. "The thing is, Sam was just a baby when it happened, and the only way he knows his father and grandfather is through these pictures of them dressed for Frontier Days. He thinks they were great cowboys and I didn't see the harm in letting him believe that. Only now Sam is convinced he wants to be a cowboy, too."

"And you don't like the idea."

"*Ohhh...*" She rubbed her forehead and sighed. "I would prefer that he was interested in something else, but if this is what he wants, then so be it. But first, he's got to see what it's like."

"A cowboy needs a horse."

She gave him a look. "Sam has been telling me that for months. My mother-in-law is horrified. She doesn't want him anywhere near a horse."

"How are you with horses?" he asked, though he'd already figured out the answer.

She was standing a good distance away from Black

Star. "I was never a horsewoman to begin with. I know the accident wasn't the horse's fault, but…" She trailed off and stared at Black Star. "Being around him is harder than I thought."

"But not as hard as seeing Sam riding him, I'll bet."

She gave him a grateful look. "He wants to learn to ride so much, and with his grandmother so opposed, it's caused problems. That's why for our date, I want you to let us come to your ranch for two weeks."

Two weeks at his ranch? Matt blinked. He'd figured she was leading up to a couple of afternoons of lessons. "Dates must last a lot longer than I remember."

"I know it's not what you expected," Jessica went on, "but I want Sam to see what it's like to be a cowboy. I want you to teach him to ride horses and…and do whatever ranchy things there are to do."

"'Ranchy' things?"

"You know…with ropes and horses and cows. Whatever you do all day."

Matt spent a considerable amount of his time repairing stuff that was broken or figuring out how to feed animals that weren't exactly native to Texas. "Jessica—"

"I'll pay you."

"You've already forked over enough cash. I'll be happy to give Sam a couple of riding lessons. No problem."

"You don't understand." She gestured with her hands. "I don't want a couple of lessons, I want the whole ranching experience. He should milk cows and…and go on roundup—"

"Roundup is in the spring."

"Well, then, fake one. He won't know the difference."

"He'll know when we don't find any calves."

"Then tell him you're taking inventory. Just go out with him and let him sleep under the stars, have a camp-fire, eat beans and—"

"Jessica—"

"I'll pay you."

"So you've said." Matt didn't like her waving money around.

"Five thousand dollars."

He couldn't take her five thousand dollars. "Sorry."

"Then I'll buy your horse and board him at your ranch. Sam and I'll come visit him."

Matt shook his head.

"Why not? You'll get to keep the money and the horse. We'll just have visiting privileges, and since you're in Texas and we're in Wyoming, we won't visit often."

Matt knew he was weakening when she started to make sense. "We're not a regular ranch," he said heavily. He was tempted, and not only by the money. Jessica had been throwing "we" around. That meant she would expect to come along, too.

Jessica Fremont at Winter Ranch for two weeks was a dangerous thing. The more Matt was around her, the more he found to admire. After two weeks of admir-ing…well, it would be hard to say goodbye.

It was going to be surprisingly hard to say goodbye as it was.

"Look, I'm not expecting 'Dallas,'" she said. "I just want Sam to ride a horse, see some cows up close, and maybe have a hayride."

"We're not a dude ranch, either. But you know something? A dude ranch is exactly what you need."

"A dude ranch won't have you and Black Star."

Matt was flattered to be included. "How about if I plan to stay on here a few extra days—"

"Ten thousand."

He shot a look at her. "Money doesn't mean much to you, does it?"

Her face was set. "Of course it does. It's just that my son's happiness means more."

Ten thousand dollars was a powerful lure. Everything in him was screaming, "Take it!"

It was a lot of money to Matt and obviously not more than pocket change to Jessica. Still. "That's way too much money, Jessica."

"It's fair. I'm preventing you from selling your horse, so I should cover your financial loss. And this way, you wouldn't have to sell Black Star, would you?"

Matt exhaled and drew his hands to his hips. "You fight dirty."

She smiled. "I'm desperate. Please?"

Matt turned away, but Jessica stepped in front of him. "I'd promised, *promised* Sam he could go to a horse camp this summer, and this morning, my mother-in-law fixed it so he couldn't. I told him I'd make it up to him. Please help me keep my promise to my son."

A mother's promise. Matt remembered a hundred promises his mother had made to him, all of them broken. She'd never seemed to mind, not like Jessica.

But he had.

"Okay," he said simply.

He wished he didn't have to take her money, but he'd made some promises of his own.

CHAPTER SIX

LIZ AND TARA'S PRESENCE allowed Rachel to have some cooling-off time, but the sisters left early the next day and Jessica knew her mother-in-law was still simmering.

"Bye, hon." Liz hugged her. "I'm sorry I didn't get one of those bachelors, but I know you're going to have a real good time. Since you've been out of circulation so long, I left you a little present in your purse."

"What?" At their knowing looks, Jessica's mouth dropped open. "You mean a...a..." She looked around to see where Sam was.

"Condom. You can say it. It's responsible."

"You left her just one?" Tara asked.

"For the man she bought? Of course not."

Laughing, they waved goodbye.

Jessica could feel her face heat and hoped Rachel hadn't heard.

But even if she had heard, Jessica was in just the sort of rebellious mood to leave Liz's present exactly where it was.

Rachel was waiting for Jessica in the kitchen. A cup of coffee sat untouched by her elbow.

"Are they gone?"

Jessica nodded.

Rachel drew herself up in the chair. "How could

you? How could you drag the Fremont name through the dirt?''

Jessica let her get it all out of her system. When Rachel finally quieted, Jessica informed her that she and Sam were going to spend two weeks on her bachelor's ranch in Texas.

Rachel hadn't spoken to Jessica since.

Every penny she'd spent was worth it, Jessica had to remind herself several times a day during the next couple of weeks.

I'm doing the right thing.

Sam was beyond ecstatic. Rachel was beyond angry.

Jessica was beyond frazzled. The emotional strain between the three of them was wearing, but in addition, she had to prepare to take vacation from Fremont Construction.

In all the years since she'd worked there, Jessica had never taken more than part of a day off, usually to go to a function at Sam's school. Now she had to delegate a number of her duties, though she planned to remain in touch by phone.

She and Sam left for Winter Ranch early the morning after school was out. Jessica chose to drive. They could have flown and rented a car, but she wanted the time alone with her son. She'd bought some sing-along tapes and planned some side trips to caves and Indian ruins.

It would be a time to reconnect and to strengthen the fraying bond between them.

Naturally this idyllic plan was doomed by the reality of endless hours cooped up with a nine-year-old boy.

Sam informed her that the tapes were for babies and he didn't care about caves or educational side trips climbing ruins. He wanted to get to the ranch and see Matt and Black Star and told her so endlessly.

So Jessica just drove and hoped Matthew Winston could stand being up on a pedestal for two weeks.

"NOBODY WANTED TO BUY Black Star? Are they crazy in Wyoming?" Frank had been at the barn when Matt arrived back at the ranch. Given the time of day, Matt was immediately suspicious.

He'd opened up the trailer and was backing out Black Star. "Best I can answer you is yes, I had some serious offers for Black Star, but I didn't sell him—"

"Ha! You couldn't go through with it. I should have known."

Matt could have, and would have, sold Black Star, but he didn't mind admitting that he was glad not to. "And yes, I firmly believe that folks are a little crazy in Wyoming. They're certainly a different breed."

"Ah." Frank blocked the entrance to the horse stalls. Matt had been leading Black Star in that general direction and was forced to stop. "What is it, Frank?"

Frank rubbed his hands together. "It is like this, Matthew. Black Star, he is such a fine horse, I expected you to have no trouble selling him, and thus a vacancy occurred in our happy family."

"Frank!" Matt stepped around him and pulled open the double doors.

A zebra now occupied Black Star's stall.

"What is that lovesick zebra doing in here?"

Frank's mustache quivered. "It would make a person cry."

"I understand that sentiment completely."

He gestured. "They are so happy now. Like Romeo and Juliet. Antony and Cleopatra. Marco, the living skeleton, and Butterball Betty, the fat lady."

All doomed relationships just like this one. Matt exhaled. "We're talking about a zebra and a mule!"

"Matthew, have you no heart?"

Behind him, Black Star snorted. Shelby, the zebra, and Tobias, the mule, looked at them soulfully.

Soulfully? Frank was getting to him. "Shelby and Tobias have had their fling and it's time for her to go home."

"True love can't be denied," Frank said.

"Sure it can. It is every day." Matt led his horse away and climbed into the truck to get the saddle. "I'm going to exercise Black Star. In the meantime, I want you to muck out his stall completely and scrub it down. Get rid of the zebra scent."

"We could make room in the stable."

Matt gave him a look. He didn't want to make a big deal of it, but this constant encroachment by the circus people was going to have to stop. "The wood in that next-to-last stall is still rotten, unless you rebuilt it while I was gone?"

Shaking his head sadly, Frank said, "Other things occupied my time."

Matt supposed he'd be hearing about the "other things."

A chattering sounded from the hayloft and Caesar swung across the rafters and landed on the divider between Tobias and Shelby.

"Even Caesar is pleading their case." Frank put a hand over his heart. "Let them be together."

This was ridiculous. "Frank, Black Star hates that zebra since she bit him. He barely tolerates old Toby. Now, clean up the stall!"

Matt left without telling him that Jessica and Sam were coming.

He'd probably regret that.

It was suppertime, but Matt needed a ride on Black Star as much as the horse needed to be ridden. As he rode, he saw his ranch as Jessica and Sam would see it: weathered and worn.

He knew he shouldn't be so hard on himself, but coming from Lost Springs with its abundant labor pool and fresh paint, Winter Ranch looked shabby.

The house, built of a creamy-colored native stone, wasn't so bad, though the trim could use some paint and the interior could be spiffed up some. But it was clean; Lita saw to that.

Jessica and Matt would be staying there. He'd give Jessica Barnaby's old room. Though it was the master suite, Matt hadn't gotten around to moving in yet.

Maybe he never would.

There were a couple of other bedrooms, but one had become a catchall and Lita sometimes stayed over in the other. Sam would stay there, since the bunkhouse was only opened during the winter when the circus folk's kin came to visit.

Matt rode Black Star toward the ravine that provided a natural divide along the northeast section of the ranch.

It was June and the land should be all green and grassy. Instead the vegetation was scrubby and a bare trickle of water moistened the cracked earth. Paw prints scarred the banks, including a set of huge round ones, which told Matt all he needed to know.

With the water so low, the circus animals were crossing over into ranch land. Normally he'd just ignore it, but with grazing land stressed, he didn't want to find that what cattle he had left had become dinner for the tigers.

The circus people were supposed to keep the animals

on their property. That was the deal. Matt crossed the ravine, not at all surprised to see gaping holes and trampled fence posts. He'd been known to repair the fence, himself, even though it wasn't on his side.

Once past the ravine, Matt entered the cluster of homes by the back way. He rode past the animal pen that marked the dead end of the dirt road leading from the highway about a mile up ahead.

The pen was empty. Great.

Matt walked Black Star along the road, peering into the wooded area lining it. Several mobile homes sat on the right, a few free-standing houses were scattered to the left. Old traveling circus wagons parked here and there added a splash of color. He could hear the laugh track from some TV show, and the incessant clank from Tom Andersen's iron workshop sounded in time to Black Star's gait.

The whole community looked like a retirement village, which was what it was, he supposed.

About thirty years ago, the circus people had built a large warehouse to store tents and props during their off season. The structure had been added to now and then and currently served as a community center.

Matt headed here, looking for Krinkov, who'd been the owner of a Ten-in-One, a collection of traveling carnival acts, and was more or less in charge when Frank wasn't around.

Matt found him playing cards with Rafael, a former sword swallower, and Dominic, the human pin cushion. After a glance around to see if any animals lurked in the shadows, he dismounted.

"Matthew! You still have your horse." Krinkov gestured to the other men. "Did I not wager as much? And would no one wager against me?"

The men shook their heads.

Krinkov smiled at Matt, his lips barely visible through his long gray beard. "You owe me fifty dollars for the lost wager. But since you are my good friend, I will give you a chance to win it back and more."

Heedless of the game in progress, he gathered the cards, shuffled them and fanned them out across the folding table. "Name a card. If I don't pick it, then I will give you a hundred dollars."

Matt dismounted and glanced at the cards. "Tell you what. You tell *me* a card, and if I pick it, then you keep the animals on this side of the ravine."

Krinkov narrowed his eyes. "Ace of Hearts."

Matt stared at the line of red and white patterned cards. "It's not here. There are only fifty-one cards on the table."

With an imperceptible movement, Krinkov produced the card. "Barnaby taught you well." He gathered up the deck, shuffled and redealt, unperturbed at being caught cheating.

Neither did the others seem to mind that they were playing with marked cards.

Whatever. "Now about the animals," Matt began, knowing he would encounter indifference. "You're going to have to keep them over here. I've got visitors coming to stay for a couple of weeks. A woman and her son. I don't want them frightened."

Their mood changed in an instant. "Matthew!" Krinkov stood and enveloped him in a bear hug. "For years we have wanted you to bring a wife to the ranch."

"She's not—"

"Katya!" Krinkov shouted over his shoulder to his wife. "Matthew has found a woman."

"It's not like—"

Dominic and Rafael congratulated him by shaking his hand and pounding him on the back.

In the meantime, tiny Katya came hurrying over. She'd been gardening on one side of the building while Carmen, Frank's wife and her arch rival, had been gardening on the other.

It was a flower war where everybody won.

"Matthew, such wonderful news." She pulled off her gardening gloves and plopped them on the cards. Again, no one seemed to mind.

"How did you meet your woman?"

Matt looked at the tiny woman and the smiling men. There was just no way to explain without them reading more into Jessica being at the ranch than there should be.

"Give me your hand," Katya demanded imperiously in her singsong voice.

Rather than argue, Matt obediently held out his left hand.

Katya peered at it. "Matthew, Matthew." She beamed, her face creasing into a hundred lines. "She may be the one. I see—"

"Get away from him, you old fraud!" Carmen walked as fast as her considerable girth and the cup of hot tea she held would let her. "You aren't needed. Here, Matthew. Drink."

With his free hand, Matt accepted a mug with tea leaves still swirling. They'd barely had time to dye the liquid a pale amber.

"Drink!"

One didn't argue with Carmen, either. Black eyes flashing, she glared down at Katya.

The tea was still close to boiling and Matt blew on it. Carmen frowned.

"Don't make him burn his tongue when his hand will tell us all we need to know," Katya scoffed. "I see a child."

"A child? A child?" Carmen jerked the tea from Matt and stared into the cup. She made a disgusted sound. "Drink more."

"Matthew did mention a child," Krinkov confirmed, and Katya rewarded him with a sweet smile.

"Is this so?" Carmen asked.

Matt nodded and sipped.

"Old fraud," she said to Katya. "You were weeding your puny flowers right there and heard."

Matt managed to gulp down enough hot liquid for Carmen to read the tea leaves. He swished around the dregs, then emptied the cup, holding it for a moment, before handing it to her.

Carmen was silent for so long Matt began to feel apprehensive, even though he didn't believe any of this fortune-teller stuff.

"Well." Carmen glanced at Katya. "Maybe you aren't such a fraud."

"You saw her, then." Katya smiled triumphantly.

Carmen nodded, her chins jiggling. "Come, Matthew. Tell us about your woman."

"THAT'S IT, MOM!" Sam shrieked, and pointed to an ornate iron arch over the entry gate by the highway.

Jessica would have stopped even if Winter Ranch hadn't been clearly spelled out.

The arch was a gorgeous piece of work, obviously custom. She stopped the car and got out.

"What are you doing?" Sam asked.

"I want to take a look at the arch close-up."

"*Mom.*"

"Come look, Sam."

There was a Noah's Ark-type parade of animals winding around the letters and detailed scrollwork in the columns on either side. Each column was different and adorned with what appeared to be symbols. They might have been cattle brands, but Jessica didn't think so.

What she did know was that she wanted to track down the artist who did this work.

One of her jobs at Fremont Construction was to maintain a list of artists and craftspeople who could make the custom architectural details for which the firm was known. This ironwork was superb. She knew of three immediate commissions she could get for the artist.

"Mom!" Sam pulled her back toward the car.

"Okay, Sam. Remind me to ask Matt about his entry arch." Not that she'd forget.

Jessica drove over a cattle guard and followed an unpaved road toward a line of trees that hid the land behind them and provided some privacy from the highway. Just above the tops, she could see a windmill and hoped that meant she'd find the ranch house soon.

About halfway through the trees, the road split to the right. An iron column bearing symbols like the one on the main arch marked the smaller road. Jessica slowed, then decided to stay on the larger road.

Once on the other side of the trees, she saw a cluster of buildings and figured she'd guessed right.

"Is that Matt's ranch?" Sam sounded as though he'd found heaven.

"Must be," Jessica answered with mixed emotions. Could anything live up to Sam's expectations?

True, she hoped he'd lose interest in all things cowboy, but it was equally true that she didn't want him disappointed.

Jessica drove on past a long, wooden structure that had seen better days and metal sheds that looked as if they were held together by the rust that spread over them.

She slowly drove toward a stone house that was the best-looking building in the area. It appeared she'd found the ranch house, but where were the people? The cattle? The horses? Even a chicken would be welcome.

There was no movement and no sign that there had been any in the last hundred years or so.

She stopped the car. What now?

Sam immediately opened the door and jumped out. "Do you think they know we're here?"

"I don't know." Jessica got out and stretched her legs. It had been a long three days. They could have driven it in two full ones, but the side trips she'd planned for the first day had slowed them down. She supposed she and Sam had arrived earlier in the day than Matt had expected. Maybe he was rounding up cattle or something.

Sam ran up the gravel path and knocked on the screen door, moving from one foot to the other impatiently.

Jessica stood by the car and looked around, trying to remain upbeat, but the truth of it was that she'd expected something…more. Something like the Fremont ranch.

The main compound of the weekend ranch the Fremonts had owned was larger than this, though to be fair, they hadn't owned much land with it, and as always, the house was geared for entertaining. Matt probably owned a lot of land.

He'd admitted he needed cash, so Jessica shouldn't

have been surprised that the place could use some attention. A new roof on the building across the way, for starters. Was that the bunkhouse? And the metal storage shed—she knew that's what it was because the door was off the hinges and an old tractor sat inside—the shed was listing to the right and should be razed and rebuilt.

As for the ranch house, it was a comfortable size, especially for someone living alone, as she presumed Matt was. And how much house did a person need, anyway? Hadn't she and Rachel closed down the east wing of the Fremont house?

"Nobody's home," Sam called, interrupting her mental assessment.

Jessica reached into the car and honked the horn.

An ominous growl answered from the right.

She gasped. "Sam get back in the car!"

Of course he wouldn't. "Mom, look!" He was pointing toward the huge pecan tree.

It cast its dappled shade over a...mountain lion. Or a cougar. It didn't matter. Sharp teeth were sharp teeth.

"Sam!" she screamed, and ran around the car toward her son, who remained oblivious to the danger.

He protested as she stuffed him inside the car and closed the door, then slowly backed around, groping for the handle. Hurling herself inside, she slammed the door and locked it.

"Is that a tiger?"

Jessica had her head on the steering wheel as she gulped in air. "It must be a mountain lion."

"Sure looks like a tiger."

"That's the way the shade makes him look."

"He's not in the shade anymore."

Jessica raised her head as the tiger—and yes, it was a tiger—slowly walked toward the paddock. Fascinated, she watched the animal's loose-limbed sway as it disappeared around the side of the building, probably a barn.

Then she turned the key in the ignition.

"We're not leaving, are we?" Sam looked ready to jump out.

"There is a tiger running loose. Of course we're leaving! Put on your seat belt."

"But where's Matt?"

Jessica refused to speculate on Matt's whereabouts.

"Can't we go look for him?"

"Sam, there's a tiger out there. I am not leaving this car."

He was silent for a moment. "Do you think the tiger ate everybody?"

Jessica shuddered inwardly. "I do not think any such thing."

"Because, if he did, then he's not going to be hungry anymore and we don't have to worry about him."

"Put on your seat belt."

"What if everybody is trapped in the barn? We could use the car to distract the tiger, and then they could escape."

Jessica had the car in reverse. The smart thing to do would be to turn around and hightail it out of there.

But…but what if Sam was right?

"Come on, Mom."

The thought of being a hero in her son's eyes made Jessica drive the car past the paddock toward the barn.

She saw a movement against the wall and realized that the big cat was sunning itself, belly outward.

Okay. Jessica positioned her car between the tiger and the barn door, then blasted the horn.

The tiger flinched and looked at her. Jessica honked the horn again and held it down for a long loud blast.

And there was an answering trumpet.

"What was that?" Sam asked.

Jessica had been so startled she'd jerked her hand off the horn. "It sounded like…" She rolled down the window in time to hear another trumpet followed by shouts.

The tiger went back to sunning itself.

A second later, an irritated-looking Matt jogged around the corner of the barn, right past the tiger.

Her heart nearly stopped and all she could do was lean on the horn.

"Dad blast it, stop honking your horn!" he shouted. Well, *that* was gratitude for you. "There's—"

"What do you think you're doing? We don't have bellboys or valet parking."

This was not the welcome Jessica had expected. She glared at him as he leaned in the window, leaving his backside available for tiger snacking.

"Hi, Matt!" As usual, Sam was unaware of the emotional undercurrents. "We were trying to save you from the tiger."

Matt glanced toward the animal. "That's Sheba. She's harmless—unless you scare her by doing something stupid like honking your horn."

"I'd hoped to scare away what I thought was a loose wild animal," Jessica snapped.

There was another trumpeting roar.

"Unfortunately you've succeeded," Matt said grimly.

The shouting grew louder.

"Dok! dok!"

A huge gray shadow lumbered toward the paddock

followed by two men hurrying after it. "Scheherazade, dok!"

Jessica stared. "I realize everything is bigger in Texas, but that is the largest cow I've ever seen."

MATT SIGHED. She *would* have to arrive at this precise moment. He hadn't thought he'd be able to hide Scheherazade forever, but he sure hadn't expected to have to make explanations so soon.

"Mom, that's an elephant," Sam said, then added doubtfully, "Isn't it?"

Nobody answered him. The elephant continued tramping toward the paddock.

"Chi! Dok! Chi—chi!"

"Scheherazade, don't do it…" Matt muttered as the elephant plowed through the wooden fence of the paddock, kept going and crashed through the other side. She headed across a field, the men running after.

"Nuts," Matt said without heat.

He would have said a lot more if Jessica and Sam hadn't been there.

Jessica turned off the car engine.

In the sudden silence, Matt stared at the destruction of his paddock and wondered exactly what he was going to say to her. He wasn't angry. It wasn't her fault she'd scared Scheherazade and it wasn't the elephant's fault she associated car horns with fire alarms. He was just thankful the animal had taken off toward home.

"Wow, you've got an elephant!" Sam opened his door and scrambled out.

"She just visits occasionally."

Matt opened Jessica's door, but apparently she hadn't decided whether she was getting out yet. Couldn't say he blamed her.

"And the tiger?" she asked.

He hadn't remembered that her eyes were so blue. "You should have seen the barn rats before we got her."

"Very funny."

He half smiled and held out his hand. She took it and swung her legs out. She was wearing a short denim skirt and sandals and her legs were a golden honey color. They sure put the wrecked fence into perspective.

Before standing, she asked, "Any other wild animals I should know about?"

Matt thought about his menagerie. "I'll introduce you later."

Jessica got out of the car, but Matt figured it was only because Sam was inching toward the tiger. "Sam," she called in warning.

The boy stopped creeping forward.

Jessica raised her eyebrows at Matt.

"You caught us at a bad time," he said.

"I guess so."

She didn't say anything else.

Matt gestured. "If you come over to the house with me, I'll show you your rooms and you can get settled."

"Wait a minute—where is everyone?"

"Running after Scheherazade."

"The *rest* of the people."

Matt decided not to tell her that the two men running after the elephant only worked part-time when he could talk them into it. "Lita, my housekeeper, has gone grocery shopping in Lampasas. She'll be back by suppertime."

Jessica waited. "And?" she prompted when he didn't say anything else.

"And what?"

Glancing at Sam, Jessica leaned closer and lowered her voice. "The regular ranch hands. Are they out with your herd? You do have cattle, don't you?"

Before Matt could answer, Frank limped around the side of the barn. He stopped to scratch the tiger's belly, then saw Jessica and Sam.

"Matthew! Why did you not tell me your lady had arrived?"

His lady? Matt groaned inwardly. Nothing he'd said could convince anyone that theirs was strictly a business arrangement. He felt Jessica looking at him, but didn't meet her eyes.

"We just got here," Sam said.

"Hello, young man. I am Frank, better known as the Flying Francisco." He swept Sam a bow. "My trapeze work is legendary. You have heard of me, yes?"

A wide-eyed Sam nodded yes.

Frank gave a hearty laugh and draped his beefy arm around Sam's shoulders. "I like you. You don't want to hurt an old man's feelings. Because of that, I will tell you many stories."

Jessica didn't look at all sure she wanted Sam hearing such stories. Having heard them himself, Matt had to admit that her instincts were on the money.

"And now, you must present me to this lovely lady. Never say it is your mother."

"Yes, this is my mom."

Frank had made his way over to them. "Ah, Matthew." He took Jessica's hand and brought it to his lips. "You have done well."

"Frank, this is Jessica Fremont, Sam's mother." Matt tried to signal the old rogue to lay off, but he ignored him. "Like I told you, she bid on me at the auction and they're staying for a couple of weeks so Sam can have a taste of ranch life.''

"So.'' Still holding her hand, Frank smiled at her as though he knew a secret. "Tell me, it was the way he looked at you, yes? As though no other woman existed?''

"I beg your pardon?''

Matt muttered beneath his breath, fervently wishing that Scheherazade would pull a U-turn and distract everybody. "It was my horse, Frank.''

"That's what she told you, eh?'' He gave Jessica a look from beneath his bushy brows and lowered his voice. "That was naughty of you.''

Gently, but firmly, Jessica tugged her hand away. "Matt, could we talk for a moment?''

He'd been expecting this—not looking forward to it, just expecting it. "Sure.'' He glanced at Frank.

Frank smiled benignly.

Sam had been awfully quiet. When Jessica looked down at him, Matt followed her gaze and saw that Sam was transfixed by the tattoo on Frank's forearm of a naked woman with anatomically impossible proportions.

Jessica sent an inscrutable look toward Matt.

"Sam, how are you doing with that two-fingered whistle?'' he asked.

"I've been practicing.'' Sam blew and managed to get a little sound out.

Matt augmented it with a whistle of his own, and a horse about the size of a large dog came trotting out of the barn.

Caesar, wearing his usual red hat and matching vest, was riding her. They ought to be good for a distraction while he talked with Jessica.

"A baby horse! And a monkey! Mom, there's a monkey!" Sam looked thrilled.

Jessica looked stunned.

"That's Caesar," Matt said. "He's riding Sally. She's a full-grown miniature horse."

Caesar jumped down and came running toward them. Startled, Jessica grabbed Matt, but Frank held out his arm and the monkey ran up it and climbed onto his shoulder.

Sam was busy petting Sally.

"She's used to kids," Matt told Jessica as she released him. "He'll be fine with her."

He'd instinctively turned his body, placing himself between her and the monkey, and for a moment, she'd been pressed against him. Matt had had to force himself not to close his arms around her as a dozen sensations bombarded him at once.

The primary one was that Jessica was female. He could also tell she was slender without being bony, and her hair was silky and scented with a flowery shampoo. Her head came to a couple of inches under his chin.

She fit as though she belonged.

And this would be the only time he ever held her in his arms.

CHAPTER SEVEN

JESSICA STARED into the beady eyes of the skinny brown monkey and knew they weren't going to get along.

She had nothing against monkeys one way or the other, but this one *looked* at her funny.

The barrel-chested man with the waxed mustache fed him something, and the whole time the monkey ate it, he watched her with wary eyes, as though he expected Jessica to steal it from him.

She stepped away from Matt, embarrassed that she'd grabbed him like that. She wasn't usually the scream-and-cling type but there was something about the man standing next to her that brought out a dependent streak she didn't know she had.

"Sam, why don't you *and Frank* take Sally into the shade over there?" he said.

"Come on, Sally." Sam patted his leg as though he was calling a dog, but Sally responded.

Frank gave Jessica a look she wasn't sure how to interpret and silently followed her son and the pony. The monkey chattered at her, then jumped off Frank's shoulder.

Jessica flinched, but maintained her ground.

Matt drew his hands to his waist. "So what's on your mind?"

What was on her mind? *What was on her mind?*

Surely he didn't think he could bluff his way out of this.

"The elephant, for starters. What kind of ranch is this?"

He gazed at her before he answered, and she was reminded of Frank's words. *It was the way he looked at you, yes? As though no other woman existed?*

"We're just a small operation trying to stay in business."

"But…lions and tigers and bears, oh my?"

"You told me you weren't expecting 'Dallas.'"

"But I wasn't expecting 'Wild Kingdom,' either."

He drew a deep breath. "Some circus folk lease a wedge of land in the northeast corner. Sometimes the animals—"

A movement caught Jessica's attention. "That monkey is in my car!" She was going to have to fumigate at the very least. The most, she didn't want to think about.

Matt's jaw tightened. "Caesar! Get out of there!"

Caesar ignored him. Jessica stepped closer. "He's going through my purse!" Liz's parting gift was still in there. The way Jessica's day was going, she fully expected the monkey to fling the packets right at Matt's feet. And how would she explain *that?*

"Caesar!" Matt strode over to the car, but Caesar hopped out. Chattering, he ran away.

He was carrying Jessica's wallet. She was almost relieved.

"Frank, can't you keep that monkey under control?" Matt yelled.

"He's not my monkey," Frank retorted. "I'm an aerialist."

Matt and Jessica chased Caesar toward the pecan tree where Sam was playing with the miniature horse.

Jessica knew it was a losing proposition. The monkey scampered so fast she couldn't see his legs move.

He stopped once to chatter a taunt at them, then ran up the tree and perched on a branch well out of reach. There, he proceeded to remove her credit cards, pictures, business cards and assorted pieces of paper and drop them one by one.

"Caesar, coin!" Matt called.

The monkey dropped a twenty-dollar bill, which floated on the breeze. Except for the credit cards, most of the papers were floating on the breeze.

Sam laughed as he tried to catch them before they hit the ground. Thoroughly annoyed, Jessica chased down the others.

"Come here, Caesar!" Matt caught a video rental card.

The monkey shook the wallet and heard the change jingling. At the sound, he screeched and bit the leather.

"If you won't come down, then just drop the wallet!"

At that instant, Caesar figured out how to open the coin purse and squeaked delightedly. As Jessica watched in frustration, he hopped from foot to foot and turned around, scattering coins from the open purse in the process. When he heard them fall, he started chattering again, dropping the wallet, which caught on a leafy branch.

Screeching, Caesar ran down the tree and gathered the coins, twirling and hopping as he did so.

Jessica gave up and watched. She was not going to get into a coin-gathering competition in the dirt with a monkey.

With each coin he picked up, Caesar bit it, then put it in his hat.

"You've done this before," she said to him.

Matt overheard. "He used to make money dancing and collecting tickets for the sideshows." He handed her some stamps, a couple of credit cards and the phone number of a woman interested in building a guest cottage on her property.

Jessica sighed.

"He likes quarters best."

"It appears he likes *stealing* best." She arranged the contents of her wallet in a grubby wad.

"Sorry about that," Matt said, and Jessica had a terrible suspicion that he was finding it hard not to laugh.

Once Caesar had scoured the grass and dirt for coins, he chattered—actually more of a gloating, Jessica thought—and scampered away with his ill-gotten gains.

"Make him do it again!" Sam obviously thought the whole thing was wonderful.

"You have to say 'coin,'" Matt told him. "Then he'll dance for you. You've got to give him a coin, though, or he'll get pretty riled up."

"I never said 'coin,'" Jessica pointed out.

"I guess he was just showing you how the game worked."

"Does he treat all your visitors this way?"

"We don't get many visitors—"

"Why am I not surprised?"

"We don't get many visitors who aren't used to monkeys," Matt continued heavily.

And that pretty much said it all. Jessica stared at him, then looked up into the far reaches of the tree where her wallet was still snagged on a branch. It was so far out of reach even what's-his-name, the Flying Francisco, couldn't get to it.

And she didn't even care about the wallet that much. What she did care about was Sam. She'd promised him he was going to a ranch. Matt Winston *knew* this, yet he'd still allowed her to bring Sam to a place where there were rampaging elephants and thieving monkeys.

Jessica's ranch knowledge was limited, but she *did* know that elephants weren't normal ranch animals.

She looked around once more. No cattle. No horses— regular-size ones, anyway. No sign of ranch hands, unless she counted Frank.

This place wasn't a ranch, it was a zoo.

For this she had defied her mother-in-law?

Rachel. Jessica closed her eyes. If her mother-in-law ever found out...

"Jessica, I'm sorry about Caesar," Matt apologized. "Look, let's get you settled, and I'll saddle up Black Star and give Sam his first lesson. Everything will be okay."

She exhaled and opened her eyes. "Will it?"

"What do you mean?"

"You knew I wanted to give Sam a typical ranch experience."

"And he'll get one."

"Oh, right. Rounding up elephants?"

"There's just the one."

She gave him a look. "This isn't funny."

"I'm not laughing."

But he was. She could see it in his eyes.

If the circumstances were different, she'd laugh, too. However... "You have no idea what I went through to get Sam here—how hard it was for me to defy my mother-in-law."

Glancing over at her son, she saw that he was back petting the little horse. Good. She really didn't want him to overhear. She started walking toward the car and Matt fell into step beside her. "For nine years, I've gone along with Rachel's way of doing things because I thought it was best for Sam. And then he gets on this cowboy kick and I thought he'd outgrow it. *Hoped* he'd outgrow it, because his grandmother is so against him having anything to do with horses. But he didn't. And so I thought, fine, let him see what it's really like to be a cowboy."

They'd reached Jessica's car. "Sounds logical," Matt said. "What's the problem?"

"Other than the fact that Sam's grandmother was totally against the idea, well…" Wordlessly she gestured around them, then continued. "I'm not sure this is the right place for Sam to see what being a cowboy is like."

Matt stared at her, his eyes unreadable. Actually, right then, with his flint-colored hat, jeans, dusty boots and pale-blue shirt, and especially with that inscrutable expression, he looked every inch a cowboy.

Jessica swallowed dryly. He looked every inch a man.

A man who wasn't real pleased with her at the moment.

"I knew you should have gone to a dude ranch." Matt's expression hardened when Jessica didn't think it could. "You've got this Hollywood idea of what ranches are. You expected cowboys in full leather chaps hanging around the corral practicing their roping. You thought you'd see bronc riding and branding, and then afterward, everybody would break out their guitars for a round of 'Deep in the Heart of Texas.' Well, lady, it's just not like that."

"I *know* it's not like that. But it's not like this, either."

"It is *exactly* like this. It's drought and the highway department building right through your grazing land. It's trying to hang on to land that's been in your family for three generations by letting movie studios film on it, or selling bits and pieces of it to housing developers, or raising llamas and ostriches. It's doing anything you can to survive."

"Including letting a woman and her son come play rancher."

He inclined his head. "Including that."

He held her gaze, his own direct and unapologetic.

This man was a survivor. Even if Jessica hadn't known about his background, she'd have been able to tell. Maybe that's what had initially attracted her to him. Maybe his persistence against the odds was the quality she'd wanted Sam to absorb.

But as compelling as Matt was personally, she had to think of Sam and what he expected.

Matt had been silent, letting her think. Now he offered a half smile. "You've come an awful long way just to turn tail and go back."

True. But would Matt's ranching-reality lesson satisfy Sam? Would this ranch be so different from what he'd expected that he'd feel cheated? Jessica leaned against the car. "I don't know. I'll have to think about it."

"Well, I'm not going to stand here and argue with you. If you want to go, then go." Matt strode off.

Jessica hesitated. Why did she feel guilty? She couldn't believe she felt guilty. *She* was the wronged party here—or Sam was.

But watching Matt walk toward her son, she had a

difficult time convincing herself anybody had been wronged.

Stay? Or leave? Which? Groaning, she stuck her head in her car and sniffed. Fortunately, there was nothing but a dusty smell. Brushing off the car seat anyway, Jessica started the car and drove in a narrow arc to avoid coming too close to the tiger. The beast was still sunning herself and Jessica didn't care how tame Matt said she was, a tiger was a tiger.

She pulled the car beside the tree that still retained possession of her wallet.

Frank limped toward her. "Do you need help with your luggage?"

"Not yet," Jessica answered quietly. "I'm not sure if we're staying."

"Not staying? But I understood—"

"Things have changed."

"What things? You're angry because of the monkey?"

"No...well, yes, but that's not the reason."

"What is the reason?"

Jessica really didn't want to get into a discussion with him. "This isn't what we expected."

"Is anything what we expect?" Frank leaned against the car. "Wouldn't life be boring if we knew what to expect?"

"True, but Sam expected a ranch and I don't want him disappointed."

They both looked toward the tree. Matt was giving Sam some brown chunks, which the boy was feeding to the little horse.

Sam laughed each time the horse nibbled from his palm. Matt kept giving him the chunks until he finally shook his head.

"All gone," Sam said to the horse, and held out his hands palms up.

The horse nuzzled him. He laughed again, then as Jessica watched, he dropped to his knees and hugged the little animal.

His eyes were closed and his mouth was curved in a blissful smile. In that instant, Jessica knew her son had never been so happy.

For his whole life, she'd made decisions that she thought would lead to his happiness—maintaining a home in a place where his family had deep roots, devoting herself to grafting them both onto the Fremont family tree.

And she was going to have to make one now.

"Your son does not appear to be disappointed." Frank gave her a questioning look. "As they say, 'Happiness is in the eye of the beholder.'"

"I thought that was beauty."

"And is that not a beautiful sight?"

He was right. For now, Sam was happy. But would he be when he realized there weren't other cowboys around? Would he feel cheated?

Torn, she met the dark eyes of the man standing next to her son.

There hadn't been many men in Sam's life. A couple of teachers, the soccer coach and the cub scout leader, that was it. The rest of the time he lived with two women in a big old house set on a hill away from the rest of Lightning Creek.

Matt Winston was the first man to pay any sort of one-on-one attention to him. Was it any wonder Sam had latched onto him?

Was it any wonder *she* had?

Why else would she have bid on him at the auction?

The riding lessons had only been part of it, she admitted now. Matt had been the other part, and she couldn't take Sam away from him yet.

So, okay. They'd stay.

Besides, her driver's license was still in the wallet in the tree. It was illegal to drive without a driver's license. And just think of the horrible publicity if a Fremont was issued a ticket for driving without a license.

They'd have to stay until they could get her wallet out of the tree.

She turned off the car and swallowed.

Matt's eyes flashed and he nodded imperceptibly. "Careful that you don't put too much weight on Sally's neck," he cautioned Sam when the horse sidestepped.

Sam released her, but continued to pet her and rub between her ears.

"Sam, let's unload our stuff," Jessica called. "I hope I don't regret this," she said under her breath.

Frank opened her door. "On the trapeze, there is a moment when the flyer must let go and trust that the catcher will be there. If you wait until you see that the catcher is in place before you let go, then it is too late and you will fall." He eyed her approvingly. "You would have made a good trapeze artist. You have let go and now you must trust that Matthew will be there to catch you."

JUDGING BY THE BUILDINGS in the ranch yard, Jessica didn't have high hopes for the interior condition of the modest stone building, so she was pleasantly surprised to find it comfortably, if masculinely, decorated, with no sign of animals running loose inside.

They got Sam settled in a small, plainly furnished room and Jessica told him he had to unpack and put away all his clothes before he could go back out and play with Sally.

When she and Matt left him, he was already shoving his T-shirts into a battered dresser.

"You'll be staying in here." At the opposite end of the hall, Matt indicated a room that was obviously the master suite.

The furniture was a heavy dark wood echoed by the exposed beams in the ceiling. Nice architectural detailing, Jessica thought. An open door led to a bathroom. "This must be your room. You don't have to give up your room for me."

"I'm not. My room is next to Sam's." Matt leaned against the doorjamb, filling the space. "This was Barnaby Schultz's room. He owned Winter Ranch until he died about a year and a half ago, and I haven't felt like moving in. Doesn't seem right."

"I know what you mean." Jessica felt him look down at her. "I was never able to move into the president's office at Fremont Construction after my husband died. I gave it to the crew manager and took a different one."

"You...go to work there?" Matt carried in her suitcases and set one on the trunk at the foot of the bed.

"I sure do. Boggles the mind, doesn't it?"

"I apologize for saying so, but yes." His gaze swept over her. "You don't seem the type."

Jessica wasn't offended. "Fremont Construction is Sam's legacy. Rachel and I wanted to keep it going for him." And working there had given her something to fill the lonely hours. She laughed. "I never expected to enjoy it, but I do. Speaking of which, is there a phone jack in here?"

Matt gestured. "Over by the night table."

When she got farther into the room, Jessica saw the

basic black dial phone. "Will my modem work out here?" she asked.

"Set your modem software for pulse instead of tone. That's what I had to do."

"You've got a computer?" That was unexpected.

"Not the latest with all the bells and whistles, but yes. I use it to track cattle."

"You're kidding."

Matt shook his head. "I have a list of my cattle with the calves I've had from each and their birth weight and so on. When I have to cull the herd, I can look up their stats and get rid of the least profitable ones."

"So you do have cows around here somewhere."

"Not as big a herd as we had a few years ago, but I can manage to scrounge up a few for Sam."

"Listen." Jessica set her laptop and purse on the bed and turned to face Matt. She caught the full force of his gaze and was momentarily distracted. When a person had this man's attention, she had *all* his attention.

Jessica made herself say what had to be said. "Right now, Sam is happy and that's the most important thing. I think we got off to a bad start and I'd like to start over."

"Fine with me." Matt gave her a half smile that slid into a full one.

His face, which wasn't exactly cracking mirrors to begin with, ratcheted up another couple of levels on the attractiveness scale. Jessica felt the bed against her calves and clutched at the brown-and-cream quilt to steady herself.

Her reaction was ridiculous. Anyone would think a handsome man had never smiled at her before.

"So tell me why you've got almost every kind of

animal but ranch horses in your barn,'' Jessica asked, trying to regain control.

"I borrowed Sally from her owners for Sam,'' Matt explained. "I noticed that he was nervous when he rode Black Star, and then after you told me what had happened to his dad, I thought maybe Sally would let him get used to horses gradually.''

"It was a good idea,'' Jessica managed to reply. Her voice almost sounded normal.

"I thought so,'' he admitted. "Then there's this zebra in love with my mule. She keeps sneaking over here. And you met Caesar and Sheba.''

Jessica nodded.

"Well, Scheherazade—that's the elephant—missed her friends and came over here to visit.''

"And that's when I arrived?''

Matt exhaled. "No, you got here after she tried to get into the barn by making her own entrance. She knocked a hole large enough for Shelby—''

"Shelby?''

"The zebra. The hole was big enough so Shelby could get inside with Tobias.''

"The...mule?''

Matt nodded. "Black Star doesn't get along with Shelby, so I was trying to get her out of the barn, and *that's* when you got here.''

"And honked the car horn.''

"Yeah.'' He stared into the distance and Jessica could tell he was thinking about the ruined paddock. "Scheherazade was in two circus fires and unfortunately associates horns with the fire alarms,'' he explained.

"I am *so* sorry.''

He shook his head and gave her another quick smile.

"You couldn't have known." He gazed at her a moment—long enough for her heart to pick up speed—then said, "You need to unpack, and I need to see what it's going to take to repair the barn and fence."

He was all the way to the door before Jessica found her voice. "Wait. I can help you."

Matt looked doubtful.

"Job estimates. It's what I do." She picked up her laptop. "I don't know the local supply costs, but I'll be able to tell you what you need and the man hours required to make repairs."

Her offer earned her another smile. "Okay."

She was becoming addicted to Matt's smiles.

Together, they walked out of the house to find that Sam had somehow sneaked past them and was playing with Sally.

Frank sat on the ground, his back leaning against the tree, his hat low over his eyes.

Caesar ran back and forth, exhibiting the classic signs of jealousy.

"Coin," they heard Sam say.

Caesar crept closer.

"Coin," Sam repeated.

Caesar gave a funny hop, then twirled around before approaching Sam with his hand outstretched. Sam got to his feet, dug in his pocket and handed Caesar money.

Caesar bit it, then chattered and ran away.

Sam went back to playing with Sally.

"Interesting place you've got here, Matt," Jessica said.

"It's home," he replied.

And for the next two weeks it would be her home, as well.

CHAPTER EIGHT

THEY NEVER MADE IT to the barn. Word of Jessica's arrival must have spread because an ancient black pickup truck chugged noisily down the dirt road toward them. Following it was an old wood-paneled station wagon that still had racks for surfboards on its roof.

Lita was back and...good Lord A'mighty, Carmen and Katya were in the truck. Together. And both were still breathing.

So much for Matt's truce with Jessica. A little while ago, she'd been seconds away from driving off. He wasn't sure what had changed her mind, but was glad she'd decided to stay.

Now he had to deal with these two.

The station wagon turned into the garage and the truck coughed to a stop by the tree.

"That would be Lita." He gestured to the wagon. "And it looks like Frank's wife has brought Katya in the truck with her." Matt hesitated then said, "They're going to want to meet you."

"Sure."

"Jessica..." He wasn't sure how to warn her. But then, she'd met Frank. Maybe he wouldn't have to.

She gazed up at him, her eyes full of amused understanding. "Don't worry. I'll take everything they say with a grain of salt."

"You'll need a whole shakerful."

"Really? What did you tell them?"

Matt rubbed beneath his hat brim, then settled it more firmly on his head. "Trust me. It doesn't matter."

Lita, her arms full of brown grocery sacks, got to them first. "What is your woman doin' here already?"

Jessica's eyebrows rose.

"I had to hear about it from them two." Matt's housekeeper jerked her head toward the black pickup.

Katya and Carmen were emerging from the truck, their bearing regal and full of purpose. Matt started to sweat.

He cleared his throat. "Lita, this is Jessica Fremont. Her son, Sam, is over there playing with Sally."

"I see 'im." Lita was a sturdy woman. She'd traveled a lot of miles on the road of life and it showed in both her face and her manner. "Have you been in my kitchen?"

Jessica shook her head.

"Good. I don't want you messin' around in my kitchen."

"I wouldn't dream of intruding in your domain unless invited," Jessica said, sounding as aristocratic as Matt had ever heard her.

"I ain't gonna invite ya." Lita carried the groceries into the house.

With a fixed smile, Jessica turned to him. "The gruff housekeeper with the heart of gold?"

"Just the gruff housekeeper."

"Ah."

Audible squabbling drew their attention to the two women who approached.

Carmen was wearing her usual black, but her iron-gray hair was piled on top of her head and held in place with the antique tortoiseshell combs that were her prized possession. She'd brought her special tea-leaf-reading china cup with her in its elaborately painted box.

Katya had gone full-out in her long purple skirt with the embroidered apron and matching head scarf. Long ago, she and Krinkov had decided that they trusted solid gold more than banks. Judging by all the rattling and clanking as she walked toward them, she'd decided to wear her entire life savings in honor of the occasion.

Even though he dreaded the coming confrontation, Matt was touched that they'd made the effort to dress up.

"It's too bright out here to see her aura," Carmen was saying.

"I don't need to see her aura, I need to see her palm," Katya retorted. "You just want to get her inside so that you can force her to drink that swill of yours."

"Old fraud." Carmen pasted a gap-toothed smile above her generous chins. "Matthew, you did not tell us she had arrived."

"If you could actually see anything in the tea leaves you would have known." Katya smiled even wider, showing off her impossibly white dentures.

Matt introduced everybody, wondering just who to protect from whom.

"Let me see your left hand." Though Katya was still showing her teeth, it sounded like a demand.

"I'm not married," Jessica murmured.

"I know that, child."

"She has no ring, of course you know it," Carmen scoffed. "Everybody knows it. Come, Matthew. Let us get inside out of the heat."

"Yes," Katya readily agreed, to Matt's surprise. Those two rarely agreed on anything. "It's so hot, she won't be wanting to drink tea."

The look on Carmen's face left no doubt that refusing tea was not an option.

"I think afternoon tea is a lovely custom," Jessica said, moving toward the house. "In fact my mother-in-law has frequently said that if men practiced it more often, there would be far fewer wars. Make them balance a cup of boiling water on their laps and they'd behave much more civilly to one another."

As Matt grappled with this image, they all moved into the den. But instead of sitting on the leather couch there, Carmen headed for the kitchen and everyone followed her.

"So." Lita guarded the doorway. "You're gonna mess up my kitchen. I knew it." She nodded toward Jessica. "Anybody can see that one needs food."

Matt thought Jessica looked just fine, but his life wouldn't be worth two bits if he said so in front of the others.

"Out of the way, Lita," Carmen ordered. "We have business to attend to."

Silently Lita moved to the side. Behind her, the scarred kitchen table was already set with cups, napkins and a generous plate of gingersnaps.

Matt tried to get close enough to Jessica to warn her to avoid eating them if she had any shaky dental work, but couldn't.

A whistle from the teakettle announced boiling water. "Huh," Carmen said, and went to make her tea.

"Come and sit under the light," Katya urged Jessica.

As she walked toward the table, Matt tried to follow her, but Katya barred his way. Shaking her head, she whispered, "Spend this time with the boy. Win his heart and you've won half the mother's."

JESSICA WAS GOING with the flow.

She'd been prepared to humor the two women, anyway. And even if she hadn't, the queasy I'm - surrounded - by - females - and - something's - bound - to - go - wrong expression on Matt's face was impossible to ignore.

He was obviously fond of these women. He allowed them an incredible license, something she understood. Hadn't she done the same thing with Rachel?

"Sit," Katya ordered.

Jessica sat and obediently held out her hand. She hadn't had her palm read in ages. Now, what was the standard line? A tall, dark and handsome man would come into her life? With Matt around, that wasn't much of a stretch.

Not that she thought of him that way.

Why not? asked a faint voice within her. Jessica smiled to herself. She hadn't heard that voice in a long time.

Bracelets clinking together, Katya ran her fingers over Jessica's hand. "You have a soft palm and short nails, so I know that you work indoors—perhaps with typing?"

A fishing expedition. Jessica shrugged. "Or I could be a musician."

Katya frowned and shook her head. "There is no triangle with your life line. Besides, you have money. Musicians rarely have money unless they are famous. I have not heard of a famous musical Jessica Fremont. Therefore, you are not a musician."

Pretty good logic. "I could play piano as a hobby," Jessica offered.

Carmen laughed and swished boiling water in the teapot. Lita didn't crack a smile.

"But you do not."

Katya gazed at her so intently that if Jessica actually were an amateur musician, she'd deny it. "No." Okay, fine. She'd play along, but she wasn't going to reveal any information.

"You have had tragedy in your life," Katya began.

"Ha!" was Carmen's comment as she spooned loose tea into the pot. "She's not married and she has a son."

"There's some as what wouldn't think that was such a tragedy," muttered Lita.

"Come here, both of you!" Katya angrily jerked Jessica's palm toward them. "Do you not see the deep crease that crosses her life line?" Her heavily ringed finger poked Jessica's hand.

Carmen waved her off. "Go ahead with you. We'll see what the tea says." She removed a white teacup from a box lined with green velvet.

Her feathers still ruffled, Katya settled back into the wooden chair. "You see how the two lines are entwined there? There will be another man in your life."

"A tall, dark and handsome one?" Jessica couldn't resist.

Katya gazed at her, her eyes nearly black. "Or a short blond one who likes tiny horses."

"Oh."

"You see this?" She pointed.

Jessica saw lines. Moisturizer time.

"The lines part," Katya said.

Actually, Jessica did see a *Y* across her palm. She nodded.

"You will have to make a difficult decision soon. You will be parting ways with someone."

Maybe Katya was referring to the rift she'd had with Rachel this past week, Jessica thought before she could stop herself. Honestly, almost anyone would be faced with a difficult decision at some point. She should just humor the women and not take any of this seriously.

"When is your birthday?"

"August 17."

Katya nodded. "Leo. I see the strength in your palm."

She continued to examine Jessica's palm, though she didn't say much more, and when Carmen brought over a stark white cup with tea leaves swirling in it, she relinquished Jessica's hand without protest.

That wasn't much of a reading, Jessica thought, more troubled by Katya's serious expression than she wanted to admit.

Carmen raised her eyebrows. "Well?"

"Read the leaves."

The two of them exchanged a look.

They were spooking her. Jessica reached for a cookie. "I haven't had gingersnaps in ages," she said, trying to lighten the mood. She dunked the cookie into her tea, then bit into it, savoring the spicy flavor. "Wonderful. These beat biscotti in my book."

She thought Lita's florid face softened a fraction, but was probably imagining it. The woman did unbend enough to join them at the table.

Jessica was halfway through her second cookie when a thought occurred to her. "Will crumbs interfere with reading the tea leaves?"

Carmen shrugged silently as she set a cup down in front of Katya. Both women sipped their tea and watched her.

Intimidated, Jessica drank her tea too fast and scalded her tongue. She also swallowed a few leaves but decided not to mention that.

Setting her cup down, she asked Carmen, "Is that okay?"

"Hold the cup in your left hand with the handle positioned in front of you."

Jessica did so and noticed that the cup had strange symbols inside it.

"Swish the leaves around in your cup clockwise three times. That's it. Try to get them up to the rim without spilling."

Jessica did so, and Carmen handed her the saucer. "Now turn the cup over and count to seven."

She counted and barely got out the word "seven" before Carmen took the cup and stared into it.

"I see three," she said at last.

Katya gave a stiff nod.

Carmen's gaze locked with hers. "You said nothing of three."

"The twining was so tight, I did not notice the third line at first."

"Three what?" Jessica asked.

"You and two others," Katya answered.

"Two men?"

"Two strong-willed people," Carmen said.

"Men are usually mule-headed," Lita said.

Carmen slowly shook her head. "There is another. A very strong influence in your life."

Jessica immediately thought of Rachel, but they couldn't know about Rachel, could they?

This was ridiculous. They were guessing, waiting for her to react and give them clues.

"She, too, is strong," Katya said.

Carmen looked troubled.

Katya smiled faintly. "Exactly. I believe she bends to her own will and not another's."

"That would explain it." Carmen's brow smoothed. "And that could be good."

"Do you see a ring?"

"In the bottom of the cup," she said with obvious disappointment. "And a saw… But—" Carmen smiled at last "—I see a star. Whatever she dreams for is within her grasp."

"Then she better be dreaming for the right thing," Lita said.

They all looked at Jessica. "I…I just want to raise my son the best way I know how."

"That is good, but you want more. Your palm says so." Katya smoothed out Jessica's hand and pointed to the tiny lines crisscrossing the base of her thumb. "All those lines on the Mount of Venus tell me that you hide your feelings and true self. Is that so?"

Jessica pulled her palm away. "The world wouldn't be a very pleasant place if everyone went around revealing all their feelings without considering the effect on others."

"Did I not tell you she had bent her will?" Katya's dentures gleamed triumphantly.

Enough was enough. Abruptly Jessica stood. "Lita, could I take some of your gingersnaps to Sam? He usually has a snack around this time and he's probably hungry."

"He'll need milk." She went to the refrigerator.

Jessica took that as permission and filled a napkin with cookies.

The other two were silent and Jessica knew they were going to talk about her as soon as she left the room. Fine. Let them talk. It was just talk. They couldn't know anything from the dregs of a cup of tea and a few lines on her palm.

Lita gave her a huge glass of milk. Jessica murmured some polite nothings and gratefully escaped.

No one was under the tree when she got outside, so Jessica headed toward the barn, smiling when she heard her son's laughter.

The tiger wasn't in sight, which was a relief.

Jessica stepped inside the barn and saw the afternoon sunlight streaming through the jagged opening caused by the elephant. Unfortunately the hole was right beneath a beam, and what boards didn't break outright probably stressed the beam. It wasn't one of the main supports, or Matt would have been in trouble. Still, the damage needed to be repaired as soon as possible.

"Hi, Mom! Look what else Matt's got." Sam was sitting on the metal railing of a stall. Inside was a zebra.

Nothing surprised Jessica anymore. "Would this be the zebra who has a crush on a mule?"

"The same." Matt had propped a foot on the railing.

He was close enough to catch Sam if he fell or the zebra turned hostile, but not close enough for Sam to realize why he was there, she noted, sending him a grateful smile.

"I brought you cookies and milk, Sam." Jessica handed him the cookies first. "These are gingersnaps. You can dunk them."

"They're horse snacks!" Sam immediately held one out to the zebra. "Here, Shelby."

Matt moved imperceptibly, sliding his hands along the railing, but the zebra took the treat without incident. Sam gravely reached into the next stall and offered one to the mule.

"Would you give this one to Sally?" Sam gave Matt a cookie and he reached over to the little horse in the stall next to the mule.

"Does Lita know you feed her cookies to the animals?" Jessica asked.

"Hope not." Matt gave a wry grin.

"They're good."

"You ate one?" he asked in surprise.

"Two, actually."

"You must have great teeth."

Jessica laughed. "The cookies are meant for dunking. If they were any softer, they'd fall apart in your milk. Or in my case tea."

"So you drank the tea," Matt said. "And you're still speaking to me."

"Had my palm read, too."

"How did it go?"

"I'm entwined with strong people."

"I'm entwined with nobody yet."

She slid a glance toward him. "I think they're working on that part."

"You noticed."

Jessica leaned against the railing, watched Sam dunk cookies and alternately share them with the zebra and mule, and vowed not to tell him he should wash his hands. "I didn't see any other wallets stuck in the tree, so I'm guessing you don't invite women here often, do you?"

"Very funny."

"Do you?"

Matt shook his head.

She smiled and patted him on his arm. "It's probably for the best."

He grinned and leaned against the railing. "I'll point out that you invited yourself."

Technically she had. Jessica thought about that. "I

can see that people have a tendency to do that to you. The animals, too.''

"I don't mind," he said quietly. "I'm grateful to have a place they can come to." He gazed around the barn. "Be nice if it were in better shape." He pointed to the last stall against the back. "Had a leak that ran right down the rafters and rotted out this whole back section before we realized it.''

"Not to mention the, uh, elephant damage.''

"Not to mention it." He squinted at the hole. "Too bad she didn't go for the rotten part.''

The entire structure wasn't in the best condition, but Jessica figured he already knew that. "See the beam that runs across the top of the loft?" She pointed. "I'd need a ladder to check it, but it's been stressed by the damage. You should get this fixed pretty quick, especially if the other end of it is rotten. I left my laptop in the kitchen, but I can give you an estimate on repairs.''

Matt shook his head. "Thanks, but—''

"No, I want to," Jessica interrupted. It was suddenly important that she show him she had some skill. "I'm really good at this. For some reason, I have a knack for estimating materials and labor. Back when we were first married and couldn't stand being apart for a minute, I used to follow Sam's father around to the various construction sites.''

He turned to face her, still leaning against the railing. He looked at her for several moments. "I can't visualize you doing that.''

His assessing gaze had an unsettling effect on Jessica. "Try visualizing me in my gold hard hat with my name in script.''

He laughed.

"Hey, I'm proud of my gold hard hat. The crew manager gave it to me the first time they sent me out on my own.'' Earning the respect of the Fremont personnel had meant everything to her. ''Anyway, my estimates were always as accurate as Samuel's were.'' She grinned. ''Even more so on the interior remodeling jobs because I knew to allow time for the clients to change their minds at least once if they'd picked some strange color or fixture.''

Matt gazed at the damage. ''Patch the hole and paint the barn white. Not much chance of me changing my mind.''

''Sure you wouldn't like a red barn?''

''White paint is cheaper and doesn't fade like the red.''

Jessica nodded absently as she walked over and examined the stall with the rotten wood. She'd have to factor in roof repair, too. ''I don't know what local labor and materials run, but I can give you a rough estimate based on what it would cost in Wyoming.''

''Labor will be free. We've got some experienced canvas men over in the village.''

''I'm sorry?''

''Old carny hands. They'd set up and break down the sites. This is nothing for them.''

Jessica mentally added another four man hours of labor. ''I'm guessing that it was their elephant.''

''Yeah.''

''Do you want posts and boards to repair the fence, too?''

Matt nodded. ''Especially if I'm giving Sam riding lessons.''

''Where is Black Star?'' Jessica was surprised Sam seemed content with the zebra and the mule and little

Sally. She'd thought he'd be after Matt to let him ride the horse.

"Out back in the holding pen. He hates the zebra."

There were plenty of empty stalls in the barn and Jessica guessed that the ranch had once been much bigger.

An unwelcome chattering sounded from above them. "Oh, great," Jessica muttered.

"Mom, can I have some money?" Sam asked immediately.

"I don't have any change," Jessica reminded him as Caesar climbed down and perched on the railing.

"Here." Matt dug into the pocket of his jeans.

There was nothing out of the ordinary about what he did, but Jessica found her eyes drawn to him, specifically to his jeans and the way he looked in them.

Noticing broad shoulders was one thing. Noticing how a man filled his jeans was another. *Admiring* the way he filled them was definitely something else altogether.

And was it so bad? Jessica let her gaze linger.

Matt handed Sam a few coins, then held out his hand to Jessica.

"That's all right. I don't mind losing some change."

"Better take them. Caesar can be a pest."

"Then I shouldn't encourage him."

"You do whatever you think is best." Matt took her hand, dropped the coins into it and closed her fingers over the change. "But when you're about to go crazy, you'll have these."

"Coin!" Sam shouted gleefully.

The monkey sidled toward him and hopped from foot to foot.

Maybe he'll fall off when he does the spinning bit,

Jessica thought hopefully, but Caesar was more agile than she gave him credit for. He turned around without falling and held out a hand to a delighted Sam.

Biting the coin, he scampered back onto the rafters and disappeared out the vent in the top.

"Where does he keep his stash?" Jessica asked.

Matt shook his head. "I've never been able to find out. I tried following him, but he won't leave until no one's watching him."

He looked down at her with those dark eyes of his. Probably because of her recent wayward thoughts, Jessica felt awareness creep over her and…good heavens, she was going to blush.

"Well, I'll go get my laptop and figure that estimate for you," she said, moving away from him.

At that moment, a car horn sounded a few bars from the *1812 Overture*.

"What's that?" An anticipatory grin on his face, Sam slid off the railing and ran through the elephant hole before Jessica could stop him.

"That's Krinkov," Matt told her. "He's Katya's husband. He'll be bringing something to patch this hole."

"And what did he do in the circus?"

"Fire eater and he owned a carnival sideshow. Now he's in charge of their animals."

And not doing a very good job, Jessica thought, but she said nothing as she and Matt stepped through the hole.

An old powder-blue Cadillac honked the *1812* again and drove overland, through the damaged paddock, to park by the hole in the barn.

"Why does he get to honk and I don't?" Jessica asked, not expecting an answer.

"Scheherazade likes that tune," Matt told her. "The circus played it when they shot people out of cannons."

It figured.

A man wearing loose-fitting trousers and a vest got out of the car. His gray beard and moustache were trimmed and curled, making him look courtly and old-fashioned.

Telling the two men in the back seat to untie a hunk of brown canvas from the roof of the car, he gestured to the barn. "Matthew, what a mess, eh? But enough of that. Present me to your woman."

Courtly or not, Jessica had ignored the "your woman" bit long enough. "There's been a misunderstanding. I'm not anyone's 'woman,'" she said after Matt had introduced her and Krinkov had brushed his moustache against the back of her hand.

"I should hope not. Matthew is an honorable man."

"Jessica brought her son to visit the ranch," Matt said heavily.

"Well, of course! You must court him, as well."

"No one is courting anyone," Jessica insisted.

Krinkov chuckled. "Matthew, she is impatient. You must begin your courtship at once."

The *1812* sounded again and they all looked toward the Cadillac. Sam had reached inside and was honking the horn.

"Sam!" Jessica waved him away from the car.

"The boy will help us hang canvas over the hole. Matthew, you will walk your lady back to the house. Take the long way."

Oh, good. She'd been upgraded to lady.

"You, boy!" Krinkov gestured to Sam. "We need your help over here."

Sam ran over to the men who were unfolding the

canvas. One of them said something to him, and Sam carefully walked along the seam to the middle and picked up the edge of fabric. All three carefully unfolded the final third.

"He'll be all right with Krinkov," Matt said to her. "Shall we?" With a smile, he offered her his arm.

Jessica took it. "I get the idea that arguing with them is fruitless, right?"

"Pretty much."

They walked around the side of the barn and encountered Frank, who was carrying an assortment of tools. "And so it begins, eh?" He winked broadly.

Jessica withdrew her arm as soon as he limped past them. "I'll go on back to the ranch house and get that estimate for you."

MATT KNEW HE SHOULD probably let her go and do just that, but he didn't want to. "You can do that," he said, "or you can spend a few more minutes walking with me and save me a lecture from Frank on how to woo a woman."

"Oh, poor you." Jessica laughed but she stayed with him.

She'd been a good sport about everything—better than he had any right to expect.

"Does he lecture you often?"

Matt looked off into the distance and smiled. "Every winter when their relatives come to visit and the circus takes a break from touring. There's always some girl they think would make me a good wife."

"And is there?"

"There was one once." He looked down at Jessica and discovered he had a hard time remembering the girl's dark hair and laughing eyes. "She was in a tumbling act—some distant branch of Frank and Carmen's family. But when it came right down to it, she realized that she was going to have to stay in this one place and decided she liked touring too much. A lot of the performers are like that.''

Matt deliberately steered them in the direction of the pecan tree. Sheba was off prowling somewhere and the view toward the hills was particularly good from there.

"How did the circus people ever end up on your ranch?"

"Barnaby, the man who used to own this place, invited them. He used to be an old carny man himself. Either he won this ranch in a card game or got it from his brother. Maybe both. I don't know. He was the least likely rancher I ever saw, but he seemed to get along okay."

"So where do they live? Are there many of them?"

"You passed the turnoff to their village when you drove in on the main ranch road."

"I remember seeing that. It went into the trees."

Matt nodded. "There's a natural ravine that cuts through the property, and unfortunately the highway you drove in on isolated a wedge of land off the northeast corner. That piece wasn't good for much, since it was highway on one side and the ravine on the other. Barnaby let a couple of small circuses winter there, and after a while, some of the performers retired and stayed put."

"Looks like their animals stayed put, too."

"Where else could they go? Don't get me wrong, it worked well for years because the circus people leased the land and it gave the ranch some income."

Now was another story, and one he didn't particularly want to discuss with her. Part of him said Jessica was exactly the type of woman he'd hoped he could interest in sponsoring the place as an animal refuge. The other part just didn't like asking someone for money.

They fell into a comfortable silence and Matt felt her study him.

"How did *you* end up here?"

"Barnaby had some connection with Lost Springs. If you ask me, either he was there himself or had a son there. He never said. Some of the boys would come here in the summers and earn money. He was a little strange, though, and it got so the guys wouldn't go. When I turned eighteen and left Lost Springs, this was where I headed. I knew he was having trouble keeping hands—"

"Because of the circus people?" The breeze blew her hair against her cheek and she tucked it behind her ear.

"Maybe." Matt knew it was true. How many cowboys had lost their wages gambling with Krinkov and his cronies? "When I got here there were still several hands around, but they quit, and then it was just me. When Barnaby died about a year and a half ago, he left me the ranch."

They were near the tree. He knew that the three women in the kitchen were probably watching them and debated whether or not to tell Jessica.

She was ignoring the view to talk about fence repairs.

Matt didn't want to think about any of it because the outlay was going to make a dent in an already dented bank account. "What would it cost to just patch the hole in the barn and shore up the beam?"

Jessica looked surprised. "But the wood is rotten in the corner."

How could he explain to her? He gazed at her smooth, flawless skin, the attractive blond streaks in her carefully cut hair, the pale pink toenails and perfectly toned legs and knew that, working woman or not, she'd been too insulated from money worries to understand. "It's a matter of financial priorities. Never buy new when you can patch old."

Her forehead wrinkled as she gazed over his shoulder at the barn. "You might be able to last another year if I do that, but then that whole side is going to collapse sometime. It'll cost a lot more then and there's no guarantee it won't cause structural damage to the entire building."

She was right and he knew it. Matt leaned against the tree. He should have sold Black Star. "Then when you figure the supply order, use Redmond's in Lampasas. They'll give me credit."

"Let me see what kind of a price I can get going through Fremont accounts. I'll deduct the cost from the money I owe you."

And that was another thing. This whole business of her paying him didn't sit well. Matt exhaled heavily. "About that, Jessica. I can't take your money."

"This isn't the time for false pride," she said bluntly. "You need the money."

"Maybe that's why I can't take it."

"We have *discussed* this. You would have had the money if you'd sold your horse."

Matt shook his head. "It's too much."

She eyed him and Matt realized he was getting a sample of the way she must negotiate business deals. "You helped me out of a jam. We both know that asking for two weeks of your hospitality and time is way more than the organizers of the auction intended. I admire you for honoring your commitment, but I would be uncomfortable if I didn't pay our way. Camp for Sam

would have cost about two thousand dollars plus transportation fare and expenses. There are two of us, so
double that. Call it five thousand. Will you take that?''

Two thousand dollars for a kid to go to riding camp?
Maybe Matt ought to look into a riding camp here as a
sideline.

"Deal?" she prompted.

She made it sound so logical. Even better, she'd let
him keep his pride. He'd never met anyone like her.
"You're something else, you know that?"

She smiled, revealing straight teeth almost as white
as Katya's. "I think that's the first time someone said
that to me and meant it as a compliment."

They shook hands. At the last minute Matt thought
of the watching women and carried one of Jessica's
hands to his lips. He was about to explain about Lita
and the others when he saw the expression on her face.

She wasn't laughing. Looking surprised, but pleased,
she blushed and wouldn't meet his eyes.

She hadn't acted that way when the other two had
kissed her hand.

There must be something to Frank's advice after all.

CHAPTER NINE

A LOUD BANGING and clanking woke Jessica the next morning. Sunlight streamed in the window, but it was from the wrong angle. Disoriented, it took her a moment to remember where she was. Grabbing her watch from the nightstand, she was startled to see that it was past eight o'clock. She *never* slept this late. She'd gone to bed fairly early, too.

It must have been the heavy chicken and dumplings dinner Lita had cooked last night, compounded by the stress and strain of the past week.

She felt heavy-headed, but lighter at the same time. So what if she'd overslept? She didn't have to set an example for anyone—didn't have to worry about someone talking about her. She didn't have to be the perfect Fremont, because no one here except possibly Matt even knew what or who a Fremont was.

She stretched and looked around the former owner's bedroom. The morning sunlight banished all the shadows from the dark paneled room and illuminated the furnishings. Opposite her in the corner was an interesting armoire, black with scrolling gold paint all over it. The words "The Amazing Molvano" arched over the top.

What a strange place this was, she thought, admiring the carved wooden molding around the ceiling. Beautiful work. She wondered who had done it. Adding a craftsman of that caliber to the Fremont catalog would be a real coup.

In spite of her resolve to relax, a little Fremont guilt was creeping into her thoughts. Didn't ranchers get up at dawn? Sam would be disappointed if he missed even a minute of the day. Jessica slipped into her robe and crept down the hallway to his room.

He wasn't there, but his pajamas were in a heap on the floor and his bed wasn't made.

This was lovely, she thought as she picked up after him. Matt would think she was a lazy dilettante and her son was a spoiled rich kid. This morning only, she'd make his bed. Then, they'd talk. Just because they were here and not at home didn't mean he could abandon his chores.

She was smoothing the old quilted spread when the banging started up again.

It was accompanied by curses—in German, if Jessica wasn't mistaken.

Curious, she went directly to the kitchen to find Lita beating up on the stove. She tried a few knobs, then kicked the huge old white appliance.

"What's the matter?" Jessica asked, belatedly remembering that she was wearing a robe.

"Stove don't work, exceptin' them two burners. Kickin' sometimes helps."

"I haven't seen anything that old in a long time." Or that big. Jessica figured it was to accommodate cooking for all the ranch hands. The whole kitchen looked straight out of the fifties. It might even be older than that.

One of the burners started to glow red. Muttering, Lita turned down the heat and put a covered pot on it. "Gas is better."

"I guess it's what you're used to," Jessica said.

"I'm used to a stove that don't work."

If she didn't know better, Jessica would suspect Lita of having a sense of humor. "Matt ought to get you a new one."

"I've been makin' do. You want coffee?"

"Please." Jessica accepted the mug, then asked, "Are Matt and Sam around somewhere?"

"Doin' chores."

As Jessica sipped her coffee, she got an idea. "I'm going to order materials to repair the hole in the barn and the fence. Why don't I order a new stove, too?"

Lita stared at her. "What are you talking about?"

"I'll show you. Pour yourself some coffee and I'll be right back."

Jessica retrieved her laptop, the Fremont supply catalog and a tape measure, and was back in the kitchen in time to see Lita set a gigantic cinnamon roll next to her coffee.

"I'll bet those are homemade." Jessica tore off a chunk before plugging in her laptop.

"Had to bake 'em in my oven back at the trailer. Can't depend on this one."

"We definitely have to do something about that. Have a seat."

She paged through the catalog until she found the kitchen appliances and showed Lita. "See a stove here you like?"

"What's all this?" Lita asked suspiciously.

"My company does construction and remodeling. This is the catalog I show clients. It needs updating, which is what I plan to work on while I'm staying here, but in the meantime, if you find a stove you like, I can order it, or the model that's currently available."

"You mean buy a new one?"

Jessica nodded.

Lita looked at the pictures. "What does Matthew say?"

"I don't see why he'd mind. I'm paying for it."

"Why would you do that?"

Jessica didn't know how much to say. She supposed their arrangements were no secret. She explained about the auction and touched on the financial arrangements she'd made with Matt without being specific.

Lita seemed satisfied with her explanation. Looking at the catalog, she almost reverently touched the picture of a range with a fancy grill to the side.

"Good choice. We've got one with a grill at home and love it." Jessica checked the dimensions. "Let's measure."

As Lita watched, her usually dour expression almost childlike, Jessica measured the space available for the new stove. As she suspected, there would be plenty of room left over.

Enough for a dishwasher.

And as long as she was ordering... "How old is the refrigerator?" she asked as she mentally rearranged the cabinets to accommodate both stove and dishwasher.

"Been here as long as I have." Lita shrugged. "I been cooking in this kitchen since Matthew was coming in summers back when he lived at that boys' home."

Jessica measured the space for the refrigerator. "What was he like back then?" she asked casually before walking back to the table and writing down the dimensions.

"Quiet. Serious little thing." Lita settled back with her coffee. "He coulda been my boy." She was silent, gazing into her mug. "I had a boy once."

Jessica looked up from the computer.

"Might still have one if'n I'd sent him to that place where Matthew was."

"What happened?" Jessica asked quietly, dreading the answer.

"My man beat us. I took it because I didn't have no money of my own. Then he killed our boy and I took off. Joined Krinkov's carny 'cause I knew he'd never find me there. And he didn't."

"I'm sorry, Lita." And because the words didn't seem enough, Jessica reached out and touched the work-roughened hand.

"I'm okay now. Katya, she give me this." From inside her faded housedress, Lita pulled out a heavy chain with a gold coin hanging from it. "Now, I always got somethin' what's mine. Ain't no man never gonna beat me again."

Jessica hesitated. "Was…Matt…?"

Lita shook her head once. "Leastwise, not regular. His momma just took off." After her confession, stories about a young Matt poured out of the normally laconic Lita.

Jessica got the impression of a boy, and now a man, who was caring, rock-solid and dependable. It was an appealing portrait, and she was glad to know her instincts hadn't let her down.

After they picked out new appliances, Jessica showed a fascinated Lita the Internet.

It was ten o'clock in the morning and she was still drinking coffee in her robe when Matt and Sam came into the kitchen.

"Mom, are you sick?" Sam asked when he saw her.

Jessica ran her hands through her hair. She had a feeling it didn't help. "No, I was talking with Lita and lost track of the time,'' she answered, feeling self-conscious.

She was trying very hard not to be aware of Matt, who had given her an assessing look as he went to the sink, but it had been a very long time since a man had seen her in a robe. She was more covered up than when she wore shorts, but there was something intimate about a robe.

This one was a soft, thin velour, which she liked to wear because Sam said it made her soft when he hugged her. The older he got, the less frequent his hugs were, so she wore the robe to encourage them.

She knew this robe screamed ''Mother's Day gift'' and was not the sort of garment that made a man think seductive thoughts. Still…

The logical part of her said she shouldn't be encouraging seductive thoughts, which irritated the feminine part. Jessica drowned them both with another swallow of coffee.

Matt poured two glasses of water and gave Sam one.

Jessica didn't know whether to draw attention to herself by leaving the kitchen or to stay put.

Lita was copying down a recipe for venison they'd found on the Internet and wasn't being a helpful distraction.

Sam, his face streaked with dust, gulped his water so fast that some dribbled down his chin. Holding out his glass for a refill, he said excitedly, ''We've been doing chores! Matt's going to teach me to ride Black Star now!''

Jessica's eyes sought Matt's and found him watching her over the rim of his glass as he drank. ''I thought you'd like to watch, if you're not too busy,'' he said.

That was thoughtful of him. "Yes. I'll get dressed and meet you outside."

"The store in Lampasas probably don't got raspberry vinegar," Lita said out of nowhere.

Matt blinked.

"Recipes," Jessica explained. "We can order the vinegar," she told Lita, and typed in the address of an online grocer. "I order unusual ingredients from these people when I don't feel like driving all the way into Casper. Look over their stuff and click on what you want, then I'll add it to my account."

Standing, she tightened the sash of her robe and walked as fast as she could without seeming to run away.

Yes, she was blushing all right, she confirmed when she looked into the mirror in her bedroom. She hadn't intended to be quite so *casual* around Matt, and now she was torn between trying to look really great and hurrying to see her son ride a horse.

Seeing her son took precedence. Jessica threw on some shorts and a sleeveless top and shoved her feet into sandals. Combing her hair, she pulled it back into a low ponytail. For vanity's sake, she put in tiny gold earrings, then walked back to the kitchen.

Lita had racked up a sizable grocery bill while Jessica had been gone, but she honestly didn't mind. The woman hadn't had much enjoyable happen in her life, and if a few exotic groceries gave her pleasure, then Jessica was glad to order them. She even sprang for two-day shipping.

"You tellin' me these things will come in the mail?" Lita asked.

Jessica nodded.

She stood. "I'd best thaw the venison."

Jessica started for the kitchen door, but at the last minute, she took her laptop. Sam was at a funny age. He didn't want her too far away, but he didn't want her treating him like a baby. Staring at him while he rode a horse might make him feel awkward, but if she appeared to be working, he might relax.

Matt had roped off a section of the damaged paddock and was showing Sam something about the saddle on Black Star.

That was a big horse, Jessica thought, and headed for the pecan tree. Her wallet was still up there, she noticed. It would only take a good strong wind to blow it down, but since she'd been here, the hot breeze had been gentle.

Sam was trying to mount the horse when Caesar's stupid chattering distracted Jessica.

"Oh, go away."

The monkey climbed a couple of branches and watched her.

"I don't care what Matt says, I'm not encouraging your money-grubbing ways."

The monkey screeched a loud, prolonged protest. It stopped Jessica in her tracks, and even drew Matt's attention. He and Sam waved at her. She waved back and watched Matt boost Sam into the saddle. He held the saddle horn and Matt started walking his horse in a circle.

Jessica moved into the shade, which prompted another outburst from the monkey. "Oh, come on. I'm going to sit here. If you don't like it, you can go somewhere else."

Caesar squeaked and ran back and forth on the branch.

"Why don't you go get my wallet and throw it to me?" Jessica asked him, then sat.

Caesar screamed.

Jessica flinched. The monkey was getting to her. "Be quiet! I'm trying to work."

He kept up a series of squawks and sounds that grew more and more agitated.

If she'd remembered to bring any change with her, Jessica would have relented and offered him a coin just to get rid of him. Leaning back against the trunk of the old tree, she watched Sam circle the paddock. Then she watched him do it again. And again.

After a few more rounds she opened her laptop, feeling a little guilty that boredom had overwhelmed her maternal pride in watching her son.

Updating the Fremont catalog was a tedious chore that she usually spread out over a couple of weeks in August so it could be back from the printers in September. It would be fun to get it all done by July this year.

It was pleasant working outdoors. She stopped every so often to watch Sam and Matt. Matt seemed to have an unending patience. But after fifteen minutes of circling, even from this distance, Jessica could see that Sam wasn't taking to riding a horse.

His whole body was stiff and she hadn't heard him laugh since he got up on Black Star. She waved to him once, but he was obviously too insecure on his perch to take one of his hands from the saddle horn and wave back.

She turned back to her laptop, enjoying the summer warmth and the earthy scents carried on the slight breeze. Yes, it was nice working outside.

The monkey, however, was not nice. The monkey was horrid and distracting, but Jessica considered this a test of wills. If she gave in now, the creature would torment her during the rest of her stay.

As the sun rose higher, the shade moved and Jessica shifted a little farther around the tree.

Caesar became hysterical, climbing down the trunk until he was only a couple of feet above her head and screeching at her.

Jessica moved back a little and he turned and ran to the lowest branch.

Matt was jogging around the paddock now, but Sam sat as stiffly as ever.

Jessica had been watching for several minutes when out of the corner of her eye she saw it—an orange-and-black movement through the grass at the base of the paddock fence.

Sheba. Sheba, the old tiger, the supposedly tame tiger, was stalking her prey, and judging by her eyes, her prey was Jessica.

She felt the ancestral fight or flee reflex take over as her heart began pounding and she broke out into the cold sweat of fear. Caesar's chattering faded into the background.

Instinct told her that she couldn't outrun the tiger. She wanted to scream, but at the same time, she knew it would draw Matt to her, leaving Sam alone and unprotected.

And did she want her scream lingering in her son's memory?

Without taking her eyes from the tiger, she pressed the Enter key and left a big white space in the catalog copy she was editing. "i loveyousam," she typed, forcing her fingers to move.

Whatever happened, she wasn't going to scream. The monkey was screaming enough for both of them.

Sheba had slowed her deadly advance and now crouched low.

Caesar, the bloodthirsty thing, had quieted.

Jessica fixed her gaze on the paddock. She wanted her last sight to be of her son.

"Mom!"

Matt had tied the reins to the fence and was running toward her, leaving Sam alone on Black Star.

"No!" she screamed. "Stay with Sam!"

Matt vaulted over the fence.

Sheba pounced.

Jessica saw a blur of orange and black as the old tiger landed just a couple of feet away from her.

Wildly screeching, Caesar leaped from one branch to the next.

Sheba growled and shook her head back and forth, a snake clamped in her powerful jaws.

Jessica's brain recognized what was going on long before her body did. Sheba, her foot pinning part of the snake to the ground, stopped moving. The snake quivered and the tiger snapped the head twice more, then released it.

Matt came pounding to a halt.

Nothing moved.

With a yawning growl, Sheba sank back on her haunches and licked her paw.

Caesar made a subdued sound and crept as close as he could to the snake's body without actually leaving the tree trunk. He looked at Jessica and squeaked.

"Yeah, I know you told me so," she said, hearing her voice shake.

"You okay?" Matt asked, breathing heavily.

"Technically, yes."

He nudged the snake's copper-and-black body with

the toe of his boot. "Hey, Sheba. You got yourself a copperhead. Must have been looking for water." The tiger rolled over and Matt squatted down to scratch her tummy.

Now that Matt was there, Caesar left the tree, calmly walked over to Sheba and started grooming the tiger's head.

Sheba closed her eyes and accepted this as her due.

This was all very touching to Jessica, but she had to ask. "Copperheads are poisonous, aren't they?"

Matt nodded and straightened. "If you're going to get bitten, that's the one you want biting you. It would hurt, but you'd recover."

"I'd recover." Her voice sounded very far away.

A hand appeared in her field of vision. She grasped it and tried to stand, but her legs shook.

"Take it easy." Matt slipped his arm around her shoulders.

"I've had a scare. I'm not hurt. I'm fine."

He subjected her to one of his intense looks. "Are you?"

She drew a deep breath, intending to reassure him. Her gaze locked with his. "I'm *not* fine!" she blubbered.

"Come here."

His arms closed around her and Jessica pressed her face against his chest. "I was so scared!"

"Shh."

He rubbed slow circles on her back and Jessica allowed herself to be comforted. It felt so good to be in a man's arms.

In *this* man's arms, she realized.

"I thought Sheba was after me."

"I figured as much." He paused. "For a minute I figured as much, too."

Jessica jerked her head back. "But you said she was tame!"

"As tame as a tiger gets, but I heard Caesar carrying on and saw her stalking, and you were the only thing I could see in her path." He smiled down at her.

Jessica felt the rest of her fear melt away as first awareness, then a growing desire became her dominant emotion. She was pressed against Matt's lean body and liked the way it felt. She liked the strong arms, the wide chest. She liked hearing the reassuring thump of his heart.

With his dark hair and dark eyes, Matt was a good-looking man. That, she'd already noticed. Add to it the fact that he was great with her son and inherently honest, and Jessica shouldn't have been surprised at her response.

The only surprise was what took her so long.

The only question was what she was going to do about it.

Reluctantly she pushed herself away. "I can't believe an amoral monkey and a tiger with bad breath saved my life," she said, her voice still shaky, but now probably from being in Matt's arms.

"You're giving them too much credit."

"Maybe and maybe not." She looked down at the tiger. "Your next steak is on me, Sheba."

"Mom!"

Sam's voice sounded close. Stepping from behind Matt, she saw her son trying to climb the fence. He'd obviously dismounted from Black Star all by himself.

A little leftover spurt of adrenaline entered her already overloaded system. She was amazed there was any left. "Sam, what are you doing!"

She'd started to run to him when one of those strong arms she'd admired so much stopped her. "Hey!" she cried.

"Don't be in such a hurry," Matt said.

"But he needs help."

"Not yet."

She watched Sam tug at his shirt, which was apparently caught on the wire. "He could have been hurt getting off the horse," she said to Matt as they started walking toward the fence.

"He was going to have to learn to get himself off the horse sometime."

"But he should have had more experience before he tried."

"Well, he didn't. Now he's learned how by himself. No harm done."

"But there *could* have been." Matt needed to understand this so he wouldn't leave Sam alone in the future.

He glanced down at her as he considered his next words. "Your Sam is a smart boy, but he hasn't had much experience thinking things out for himself."

Matt didn't look *quite* as attractive as he had a few minutes ago. "What are you saying?"

"He looks to one of us for permission to do anything."

"He's a well-behaved boy." Not counting running away when Matt had first met him.

"That he is, but behaving well isn't going to help him learn to survive."

"Maybe not here, but in the social circles in which he moves, behavior is extremely important." *She sounded just like Rachel.*

"I thought self-confidence was, too."

"He's only nine. He'll learn self-confidence."

"Not if you keep babying him."

"What?"

"Just back off a little—"

"Back off?"

Matt nodded. "Let Sam make some decisions for himself. Like right now, he's stuck on that fence. If we go over there before he gets himself down, then he won't have the experience of figuring out what he can do and what he can't."

As she glared at him, Jessica felt her anger grow. Even though she knew her emotions had gone ping-ponging the last few minutes, she told herself this conversation would have angered her coming at any time.

She heard footsteps as Sam freed himself from the fence and came running.

"What happened?"

"Sheba killed a snake," Jessica answered, avoiding Matt's gaze.

"Cool!" Sam ran over to the tiger, and though Jessica's first instinct was to stop him, she didn't.

"Oooh, there's guts!"

She finally looked at Matt again. "I think now is a good time for me to back off."

CHAPTER TEN

IF THERE'D BEEN A STURDY fence post around, Matt would have beat his head against it.

Jessica Fremont, who'd occupied more of his thoughts than he'd admit to anyone, had been in his arms, and what had he done?

Lectured her on child-rearing.

It was no surprise that Jessica had been cool toward him the past couple of days. It was just as well. They had about as much chance of getting together as that fool zebra and the mule.

Matt watched Sam work at the morning chores in the barn. The boy had been eager from the first, but too concerned about getting his clothes dirty. Only after Matt had assured him that his mother knew that dirt and chores went together did Sam relax.

It was obvious he'd been raised by women, no offense intended. By all accounts, they'd done a good job, but there were some things about being a man that a boy wanted to learn from males. Sam needed to learn more than how to ride a horse in these couple of weeks.

Matt walked over to him. "Good job on the mucking, Sam. I know it's not a fun job."

"I don't mind," the boy said quickly. "If the animals' stalls aren't cleaned, they're going to get sick, right?"

"That's about the size of it."

He looked worried. "I've been doing a real good job."

"I know. That's what I said."

"Well...I think Sheba's sick."

Matt had noticed that the tiger had spent the last two nights in one of the stalls, but since Shelby was determined to stay and Sally was here, he hadn't thought much of it. "What makes you think she's sick?"

"She didn't eat her food, and when I tried to clean up after her, she growled at me," Sam said all in a rush.

That didn't sound like Sheba. "Where is she?"

Sam pointed and Matt went over to the far stall and took a look.

"Hey, old girl." Mindful of Sam's warning about the growling, Matt squatted down, but didn't try to touch her.

Sheba barely lifted her head.

Matt dropped his. Nuts and double nuts. Sometimes he wondered if the struggle was worth it.

"Is she sick?" Sam asked.

"Yeah, you called it right."

"Can you take her to the doctor?"

"Tigers are special." Matt stood and managed a smile. "The doctor comes to them."

For a price. The exotic animal specialist would have to helicopter in. Well, he hadn't been out in a while, and as long as Matt was paying for a call, he probably ought to have the other animals checked out. Krinkov would complain, and Matt wasn't looking forward to convincing him the cost was necessary.

Between the hole and the fence and expensive vets, Jessica's money would soon be gone. He'd probably end up selling Black Star after all, unless something happened and the price of beef went through the roof.

"Make sure she has fresh water, and we'll keep an eye on her," he said to Sam.

"Keep an eye on whom?"

Jessica stood in the doorway, the first time she'd come out to the barn since she'd ordered the materials for the repairs. The sun behind her made her hair look almost as blond as Sam's.

She was wearing white shorts that showed off her legs and an itty bitty sleeveless red top that looked like one of Frank's undershirts would if it had shrunk about thirty sizes.

Matt swallowed, his throat suddenly dry. Must be from the dust thrown up by the hay, he told himself.

"Sheba's sick," Sam said.

"What's wrong?" Her concerned face had lost that carefully pleasant mask that Matt hated.

"I don't know," he admitted.

She came over to the stall and stared at the tiger.

Her perfume added a flowery smell to the barn. He could smell it in the house, too, even when she was sitting outside by the tree.

Sometimes, when he came back to the house to wash up for lunch, he'd go by Barnaby's old room and just breathe in all the feminine scents. For the longest time, he'd associated perfume with the heavy incense odor that permeated Katya's and Carmen's trailers.

This was different. This was Jessica.

Sam was telling her all about finding Sheba. Matt moved a few inches closer, under the guise of adding a forkful of hay to the stall.

He was close enough to feel the warmth coming from her body—or was that his body?

He relived the brief moments she'd spent in his arms,

half hoping Sheba would growl or snap and Jessica would take refuge there again.

He could see her shoulder blades above the scooped back of her top. When Matt thought about a woman, he never thought about her shoulder blades, but something about Jessica's appealed to him.

She turned to him. A fine gold chain lay across her collarbone and disappeared into the neckline. He wanted to trace it with his finger and clutched the pitchfork handle to keep from doing so. And he'd been admiring her shoulder blades.

She was looking at him expectantly. Her eyes were so blue and her mouth was just a few inches away.

"Matt?"

He liked the way she said his name. Matt and not "Mat-you" like Krinkov and Katya.

"Matt."

"Hmm?"

"I asked when you were going to call the doctor."

He should have been paying attention instead of mentally slobbering over her. "I'll need to let Krinkov know first. Sheba's his tiger."

"And he'll call the vet?"

Maybe. Maybe not. It depended on what Krinkov thought was wrong with the tiger. "I'll call the vet."

She looked worriedly at Sheba. "I came to tell you that the delivery service phoned and they can get your boards out here by noon. I thought you could get your crew here to get them started on repairing the hole, but I don't want Sheba disturbed."

"Let's worry about that later." He needed to get out of the barn before he did something stupid like trying to kiss her in front of Sam. "I'll go call the vet."

MATT PROBABLY HADN'T EVEN noticed that she'd been staying out of the way the past couple of days. But that didn't mean Jessica didn't watch him work with Sam.

From the ranch office window, she'd see them walking together, followed by the little horse, as they got tools out of the ramshackle shed she couldn't wait to raze. Matt seemed to talk a lot more to Sam than he did when she was around. She was dying to ask what they talked about, but knew her questions wouldn't be welcome.

Whatever, Sam clearly adored Matt, and Jessica was afraid this would be a problem when it came time to leave. That's why she frequently sprinkled her dinner conversation with lots of sentences beginning with, "When we get back to Lightning Creek." Sam never acknowledged her attempts to remind him that they were only here a short time, and Matt would simply gaze at her with those dark eyes of his.

And so she backed off.

Jessica had fallen into the habit of taking a morning break with Lita. She'd bring her laptop and Lita would surf the net for recipes and Jessica would stand by the window and watch Sam's riding lesson.

Yesterday, Matt had saddled the one other ranch horse and he and Sam had ridden off together without telling her where they were going. And had she complained? Sam still wasn't a confident rider and Matt didn't have a cell phone—what if Sam fell off Black Star and they needed medical help? What if they encountered another snake?

But they'd returned in time for dinner, and Sam was so thrilled with his day, she couldn't say anything to spoil it.

That night, Lita had fixed a hearty stew with homemade bread—a lot heavier meal than Jessica was used to eating in the hot summer weather, but not for two people who'd been riding all afternoon.

And this morning, it was already hot. She'd brought too many pairs of jeans and not enough shorts. How could Matt stand wearing jeans and boots?

Speaking of hot, this barn was stifling.

"Here, Sheba." Sam set a bowl of water near the tiger.

Jessica hoped the vet would get here soon. The animal really didn't look all that great. "Get well, old girl," she said. "Sam, do you know what you're supposed to be doing?"

Sam nodded, so she left him in the barn.

She hoped Matt noticed that she was leaving Sam on his own.

Before going back into the house, she stopped by the pecan tree to check and see if her wallet had fallen yet. She didn't mind the loss of the wallet so much as the hassle of replacing her driver's license.

While she was standing there, she heard the mufflerless rumble of Frank's old black truck several moments before it emerged from the trees.

Frank's work hours puzzled her. He came and went seemingly at will and had no assigned duties as far as Jessica could tell. Lita was nearly as bad, except that she came every day. Sometimes she stayed the entire day, sometimes she worked part of the day. She would either cook there or bring covered dishes from wherever she lived.

Frank pulled his truck next to the shed about where Jessica was going to have the building materials put. Never mind. She'd tell him later.

"Hello, lovely lady!" he called and waved.

Jessica waved back. Frank wasn't so bad, and he made Sam laugh with his outrageous stories.

Besides, his appreciative looks were good for a girl's ego.

She was on her way back to the kitchen for another cup of coffee, when she met Lita and Matt coming out the back.

"Lita's making a trip into town," Matt said. "Do you need anything?"

"I'm fine, thanks."

"Have sandwiches and potato salad for lunch," Lita called on her way to the car. "I'll be back later."

"Oh, goody. I can steal the washing machine." Jessica rubbed her hands together, prompting a smile from Matt.

The machine was going constantly. The ranch house didn't have a dryer, and most of the clothes hanging on the line outside the kitchen weren't Matt's.

"She takes in laundry for other folks," he explained.

Using your machine and supplies, Jessica thought, but didn't say. It wasn't her business if Matt let himself be taken advantage of.

"Just tell her if you need to use the washing machine."

"I think it's easier this way," Jessica replied.

"You're probably right." Matt seemed inclined to linger with her, ignoring the increasingly loud grunts and groans from Frank as he wrestled some piece of machinery out of the back of the truck.

"You and Lita seem to be getting along okay."

"Only because I surrendered the kitchen. Willingly I might add." Jessica laughed and noticed Matt's gaze drop to her mouth.

Did he realize what he was doing?

"You seem to have found plenty to keep you busy during the day." As he spoke, his gaze roamed over her face, and when it reached her eyes, she was flattered to see a definite interest in his.

"I brought work with me—updating the Fremont Construction catalog. Which reminds me, the iron arch by the highway entrance—where did you get it?"

"That'd be old Tom Andersen's work."

"Old? Is he still...?" she asked delicately.

"He lives in the circus village. Still works iron."

"I'd love to talk with him. I'm always looking for artisans for the catalog."

"I'm going to have to visit Krinkov later. You and Sam can tag along, if you like. I was thinking of taking Sam, anyway."

"Thanks." Jessica smiled. "I'd like that."

"Okay."

His return smile made her heart give a little blip.

He found her attractive and he was letting her know it. At the same time, Jessica instinctively knew Matt would never act on his feelings without the right signal from her.

An interesting dilemma. As she'd realized in the past month, she'd spent too much time concentrating on being Sam's mother and had forgotten she was a young, single woman.

The old impulsive Jessica was shouting, "Come here, cowboy."

The sensible Jessica reminded herself that she was a woman who owned a velour robe.

"Matthew! I'm an old man and can't compete with a lovely lady, but my back, she begs you."

Matt glanced over at Frank, then back at Jessica. Gesturing with a thumb, he said, "I've gotta go."

She nodded and watched him stride toward the truck. Midway, he saw Sam coming from the barn and waited until her son caught up with him.

Jessica sighed. There was a lot to admire about that man. If she were choosing the kind of man to become Sam's stepfather, Matt would be perfect. In fact, if she were choosing a man for herself...

But becoming a rancher wasn't Sam's destiny. Being a Fremont was Sam's destiny and it was her job to see that he fulfilled it.

With another sigh, she turned and went into the house.

FRANK RAISED HIS EYEBROW at Matt's approach. "Young Sam, go into the shed and bring the motor toolbox here."

"What's it look like?" Sam asked.

"It looks like a toolbox. Go. Look." Frank waved him toward the shed and Sam ran off.

"And now, young Matthew, you do not woo a woman in the hot sun, even one who is dressed—" Frank stopped and kissed his fingers "—*molto bella,* such as she. If it were not for my leg and my lost youth..." He chuckled. "I would demonstrate. As it is, you must listen. Bring her outside at night. Show her the stars."

"She's from Wyoming. She's seen stars."

"Who said I was talking about stars in the sky, eh?"

Matt picked up the tractor engine out of the back of the truck and carried it over to the heap they were trying to salvage. "Frank, you're going to have to drop all this wooing talk. You're embarrassing Jessica."

He gave a huge sigh. "She is there for the taking."

Matt gave him a look. "She's also there for the leaving."

"She looks at you."

Did she? He glanced toward the house, but Jessica had gone inside. "She's only watching her son."

"Matthew—"

"I mean it, Frank." He set the engine down on the bench beside the tractor. "She's leaving next week."

"And the problem with this would be…?"

He'd miss her. She'd only been here a few days and he'd miss her. But he knew her memory would fade more easily if he didn't have many memories in the first place. "Just knock it off."

If Sam hadn't been dragging a metal box through the dirt toward them just then, Matt figured Frank would have continued talking.

"You are making a big mistake, but…" Frank held up both hands.

"Then I'll make a mistake. Sam, can you hand me a five-eighths-inch wrench out of that box?"

JESSICA STARTED A LOAD of Sam's grubbiest clothes—pretty much anything he'd worn since they'd arrived at Winter Ranch—and forced herself to check her E-mail.

Each day, she'd sent a short note to Rachel, letting her know they were all right. If their parting hadn't been so strained, she would have called, but she didn't want to give Rachel the opportunity to hang up on her.

Instead Rachel was ignoring her E-mail. Jessica didn't know whether she was reading it or not. Still, she kept checking in with her mother-in-law.

No response today, either. Well, her conscience was clear. Sort of.

She'd done the right thing. She knew she had. Swiveling around in the leather chair, she looked out the window and watched Sam, Frank and Matt bending over a tractor that looked like it belonged in a museum. As she watched, Matt pointed and Sam reached inside and either tightened or loosened something with a wrench.

This was great for him. She'd done the right thing.

After checking in with her crew manager and answering the rest of her mail, Jessica got another load of laundry ready.

Once the machine stopped, she took the cloth bag of clothespins and the heavy basket of wet clothes and went out back where the clothesline stretched between two poles.

This was a lot different from using the tiny travel clothesline and cute plastic pins in a hotel bathroom. This was serious, time-consuming laundry hanging.

Good exercise, though.

Feeling pleased when she'd managed to get Sam's jeans to stay on the line, Jessica went back for her own laundry. She wasn't eager to hang up her underwear so everyone could see, but the clothesline was behind the kitchen and there really wasn't any room in the bathroom. As hot as it was, the flimsy lace should dry in minutes.

She heard laughter as she pushed the back door open with her hip. Walking around the side of the house, she stopped short when she saw Matt and Sam cleaning themselves off by the water spigot. Matt was squirting Sam, who was squealing in delight.

They had taken off their shirts and had rinsed them, but the scent of gasoline hung in the air.

''Hi, Mom!'' Sam made as if to squirt her, but a

laughing Matt stopped him. "We got grease all over us."

"So I see."

What she saw was the narrow-shouldered, little-boy body of her son and Matt, naked from the waist up.

All she could do was hug her basket of wet underwear and stare.

Here, revealed, were the strong arms that had held her and the shoulders she'd thought were good for a boy's piggyback ride. And there was the wide, solidly muscled chest she'd buried her head against.

She wouldn't mind burying her head against it right now.

Sam squirted Matt just then. He laughed and shook the water out of his hair. It dripped down his neck and ran in glistening rivulets that highlighted muscles built from work, not working out.

Jessica would probably still be standing there gaping at him if Matt hadn't spoken.

"Could you bring us a couple of towels?" he asked. "We don't want to drip all over Lita's floor."

She managed to nod. Abandoning the basket, she got two clean towels and brought them outside.

Sam and Matt were waiting.

"Here." Ungraciously Jessica stepped just within reach and thrust a towel at Matt.

She could feel him look at her as he took it. She didn't dare meet his eyes. Instead she wrapped the towel around Sam and started rubbing.

"Mom!" He pulled away from her. "I can do it myself."

She backed off and involuntarily glanced at Matt.

He was watching her as he toweled off, the strokes strong and no-nonsense without a hint of coyness.

The white towel contrasted with his lightly bronzed skin and dark chest hair. All in all, he looked like a calendar shot for cowboy hunk-of-the-month.

If he'd posed like that for the auction brochure, Liz never would have dropped out of the bidding.

He finished and draped the towel around his neck, then raked his fingers through his hair. A smile teased the corners of his mouth.

A small sound escaped Jessica before she could stop it. "You're probably hungry for lunch," she said to cover it up. "Lita mentioned something about sandwiches." She turned and prepared to flee inside.

"We can wait until you've hung up your washing, can't we, Sam?"

Sam looked like he wanted to disagree, but went along with his idol.

"Oh, this can wait." Jessica tried to kick the basket out of the way, but it was too heavy, and all she did was hurt her toe.

"Tell you what. Sam and I'll help you." Matt bent and picked up the basket.

A half-naked man was offering to handle her underwear. Under other circumstances...

"Hang up laundry?" Sam made a face.

"Really, I can do it." Jessica tugged at the basket. "Won't take a minute."

Matt silently released his hold on the basket and she carried it over to the clothesline. She dug around in the basket and hung up all her T-shirts first. *Go inside.*

Honestly, this was only underwear. Why was she suddenly so prissy about it?

Defiantly she reached into the basket and withdrew pieces of silk and lace and started pinning them up.

SAM TUGGED ON HIS ARM. "Let's go inside, Matt."

"In a minute. First we've got to get the mud off your shoes."

"I'll just take them off."

"And what about your socks?"

"I'll take them off, too."

"Then you'll get mud on your feet." Matt was stalling, but the fact was, he was enjoying the view of Sam's mother hanging up laundry.

Each time she bent down, her top fell away from her neck, though at this distance, he was only fueling his imagination. And where Jessica was concerned, he had a great imagination.

But when she stood and stretched her arms up, he didn't have to imagine the way her top pulled away from her shorts and left a slice of her middle bare.

"How's this, Matt?" Sam held out his leg so Matt could see the shoe.

"You've got a little mud left on the heel."

He was lower than low, and if he didn't watch it, Sam was going to ask questions Matt didn't want to answer.

Yeah, she was out of his league, he reluctantly reminded himself.

Then Jessica reached into the basket and started hanging up the little bits of stuff that she wore for underwear, and Matt decided he'd had enough fuel for his imagination.

CHAPTER ELEVEN

THE BUILDING MATERIALS she'd ordered arrived right after lunch.

Jessica was relieved. She could hardly look at Matt without seeing the image of his wet torso as he stood by the water spigot. Not that this wasn't a wonderful image, but thinking about Matt's chest made it difficult to maintain normal lunchtime chatter with Sam. Matt, too.

When the flatbed truck arrived in the ranch yard and honked, Jessica nearly leaped from the table. "I've got to check the packing list before I sign off on the delivery."

"How long will that take?" Sam asked.

"A while," Jessica admitted.

"Man." He frowned. "I wanted to go visit Frank's house. He said he has a friend who can stick pins in his arm and it doesn't hurt or nothing."

"Or anything," Jessica corrected.

"How about we ride over to the village?" Matt suggested. "Your mom can follow in her car when she finishes what she's got to do here."

"Is it very far?" Sam looked more apprehensive than excited.

"It's a fair piece."

"What's that mean?"

"It means it's farther than you've ridden on Black Star before."

Sam thought it over and gave a tight nod. Matt and Jessica exchanged looks.

Her son wanted to like riding more than he actually did. "Do you think...?" *He's ready?* she wanted to ask.

Matt understood. "He can do it. We're not going to gallop—"

"I can gallop!" Sam interrupted indignantly.

"Ground's too rough and cracked," Matt told him. "You don't want the horses to catch their hooves and hurt themselves, do you?"

Sam shook his head.

Clever man, Jessica thought. Matt had managed to appease them both. "How do I get to the village?"

"When you drove in on the ranch road, do you remember seeing a metal signpost?"

Jessica nodded.

"Turn right there and follow the path and you'll end up at the community center. It's the largest building around."

"Okay. I'll meet you guys over there."

IT TOOK LONGER THAN she thought to check all the pallets and pieces she'd ordered, but everything was there, and she had it unloaded in two areas—by the barn and in front of the shed. Frank grumbled about the work, especially when he saw the new metal siding for the shed. She left him covering the bags of concrete for the fence posts with plastic tarp. Jessica figured the leaky shed wouldn't keep the mix dry if they had rain.

After she was finished and the truck had driven away, she realized she'd have to change clothes for the visit. She hadn't brought any really dressy clothes but had packed a couple of casual summer dresses, and she picked one of those to wear.

She also brought her laptop, a copy of the catalog and some of Fremont Construction's promotional materials. She was eager to sign this Tom Andersen before someone else discovered him.

It was about an hour after Sam and Matt had left when Jessica found herself turning off the ranch road and following the rutted path. She was glad she had a four-wheel-drive vehicle.

The closer Jessica got to the circus village, the more evidence of Tom's work she saw. The road arch and the signpost both had strange symbols on them, which she now saw nailed to trees. Were they a warning or a welcome?

She smelled curry and wood smoke long before she found the main settlement. As she drove along, she saw trailers, RV's and brightly painted wagons, as well as smallish houses deep in the woods. She remembered what Matt had said about the circus people wintering here. It looked as if one spring, some of them had just decided to stay wherever they were.

She found the community center with no problem and parked.

"Hello, Matt's lady!" Krinkov hailed her.

Sighing inwardly, she returned Krinkov's greeting. He and three other men were playing cards on a battered table outside the center.

"Have you seen Matt and Sam?" she asked after Krinkov had introduced her to the others.

"Yes." Everyone nodded in unison.

Jessica waited, but he added nothing else. There was no sign of the horses.

"Where are they?" she asked at last.

Holding a hand of cards, Krinkov gestured down the road with his eyes.

Jessica didn't see anything and was considering whether to get back into her car and keep driving when she heard faint shouting followed by her son's laughter.

Seconds later, Sam rode into view.

On an elephant.

"Muhl, muhl!" he shouted, or at least that's the way it sounded to Jessica.

Behind him rode Matt, thank goodness, though if the elephant decided to lumber off cross-country, Jessica didn't see how they'd stop it.

A wizened man in baggy white clothes jogged alongside them. Jessica didn't think he was capable of stopping an elephant, either.

"Mom, look!" Sam shrieked.

She waved. "Not so loud, Sam," she muttered between her teeth-clenched smile. "You don't want to scare the elephant."

As the elephant lumbered ever closer, Jessica kept glancing at the men to see if it was time to panic. They ignored the elephant, so Jessica figured everything was under control.

"Dok!" Sam leaned back against Matt. "Dok! That means 'stop' in elephant talk."

And darned if the elephant didn't stop right in front of the community center. Jessica raised a shaky hand to shield her eyes from the sun and looked up at them.

Sam and Matt wore identical grins, which tugged at her heart. "So who have you got there?"

"This is Scheherazade," Sam said.

"Is it? I don't believe we've formally met. How do you do, Scheherazade?"

"Mom!" Sam laughed.

Matt smiled down at her—a wonderfully warm, intimate smile. "Want a ride?"

The sensible thing would be to say no.

Jessica didn't feel like being sensible just then.

Come to think of it, she hadn't felt sensible since the auction.

"Okay." She smiled back up at Matt.

Behind her, chairs scraped back. "You are going to ride the elephant with Matthew?" Krinkov asked.

"Yes, if it's all right." Jessica didn't understand why the man looked at her so intently. Surely it was safe if Sam had been riding.

"It is more than all right. It is past time." He went to the door of the community center. "Katya!" he bellowed. "Come, woman. Matthew's lady is going to ride the elephant with him."

Jessica heard excited feminine babble, and within seconds, Katya and several other women appeared.

What was going on? Maybe women didn't ride elephants. But Jessica had seen them do so in the circus parades.

Or maybe only a *certain* type of female rode elephants.

She looked up at Matt for some hint, but he was reassuring Sam that he could have another ride on Scheherazade later.

"Okay, then. Tell her to kneel," Matt instructed him.

"Bite! Bite!" Sam bounced up and down on the elephant's neck. "Did you hear that, Mom? It means down."

Scheherazade laboriously bent her knees. Even so, her neck was a long way off the ground. Too bad Jessica hadn't asked exactly *how* she was going to get up there.

"What is this? What is this?" Carmen stuck her head out of a huge mobile home.

"She's riding the elephant with Matthew!" Katya called.

Carmen muttered and came outside. "And where is my Frank that I should have to hear such from the likes of you?"

Jessica was having definite second thoughts about this whole elephant thing. With lots of effort, Scheherazade had finally managed to get to her knees. Jessica hated to make her go through that again. Matt held onto Sam's arms as he slid down far enough to stand on the elephant's trunk and then jump to the ground.

"Mom, it's so totally cool up there. You don't need to be scared, 'cause Matt will hold on to you, won't you, Matt?"

His dark eyes met hers. "You bet."

Some nice side benefits were associated with elephant riding.

There was a murmuring from the crowd that continued to gather. When Jessica looked at their faces, they didn't seem to be disapproving—quite the contrary.

"You've got to take off your shoes," Sam told her. "Then you put your feet behind her ears. That's how you steer her 'cause she doesn't have reins."

"I have to take off my shoes?"

Matt nodded, so Jessica slipped off her sandals.

As she did so, she heard Katya remark, "Was an elephant too big to see in the tea leaves?"

Carmen snorted. "*You* did not see an elephant in her palm, you old fraud."

"Did I not see a decision?"

"Put your foot here, Mom." Sam patted the curve in Scheherazade's trunk.

Okay. This was it. "Wait for me right here, Sam."

"I will look after the boy," Carmen announced.

"And maybe he doesn't want to go with you." Katya smiled widely at Sam, but since she wasn't wearing her good dentures, it didn't have quite the reassuring effect she must have wanted.

Sam looked doubtfully at the women.

"The boy is thirsty," Carmen insisted. "He'll want tea."

"Tea is no drink for a boy. Give me your hand, young Sam."

"He is a boy! What can his hand tell you?"

"More than your silly leaves."

"Ladies." Krinkov interrupted them. "We are keeping Matt's woman from riding the elephant with him. Young Sam, how would you like to learn the secrets of moving cards with your mind?" Krinkov split the card deck he held, showed Sam the ace of diamonds, put the deck back together and tapped the top. "Turn the card over."

It was the ace of diamonds. "Wow!" Sam said. "And I can do that?"

"Only if you concentrate very, very hard." Krinkov tapped his temple and led the way back to the table.

Once, in another life, Jessica had studied deportment. Elephant mounting hadn't been covered.

"Did you see how Sam climbed down?" Matt asked.

"Yes, but I didn't see how he got *up*."

Chuckling, Matt leaned forward so far Jessica thought he might fall off. "Put your foot on her trunk. Now, grab my hand."

Jessica shut her eyes, as well, though she probably wasn't supposed to. She felt Matt's strong hand close over hers and then she blindly grabbed a handful of elephant ear. Half walking, half pulled by Matt, she ungracefully landed stomach down on Scheherazade's back. With Matt's hands on her waist, she managed to hoist her hips in front of him in the small boxlike seat.

"Swing your legs over and you're all set."

"Easy for you to say." Jessica looked down at the waiting crowd. "How about I just ride sidesaddle?"

"You'll need to steer with your feet. Put them right behind her ears." His hands steadied her.

Or unsteadied her, depending which way she thought about it. Jessica bunched her full skirt above her knees and dragged her right leg over Scheherazade's head, feeling the sparse, coarse hair.

Matt encircled her waist and settled her firmly between his thighs. "Hang on."

He shouted something—Jessica wasn't paying attention to exactly what—that must have been a signal for the elephant to get up.

All her conscious thought was occupied by the fact that she was being cradled firmly between the strong thighs of a man whose attractiveness registered off the hunk scale.

She felt...primitive, with her bare feet and nothing much except some flimsy material between her, the elephant and Matt.

They swayed from side to side as Scheherazade got to her feet.

"Take her for a long ride, Matthew!" Krinkov shouted, and the crowd laughed.

"Bye, Sam!" Jessica called.

Sam looked up, briefly waved, then returned to the important business of learning card tricks.

"Why are they so interested in me riding the elephant with you?" Jessica asked.

"I don't know." Matt still held her tightly.

Jessica didn't mind a bit.

He leaned down. "Press your toes just behind her ear and say 'muhl.'"

She could feel his breath warm the skin of her neck and shoulder. "Muhl?" Her voice cracked.

"Say it louder and with authority. Show her you're in charge."

"*Am* I in charge?"

"On this ride you are."

"Muhl!" Jessica pressed her toes into leathery elephant skin. "Muhl!"

Scheherazade shuffled forward.

"It worked!" she exclaimed.

Matt laughed and his chest rumbled against her back. He briefly tightened his arms around her middle, holding her securely until they were well under way.

Smiling, the people followed them for a bit, then stopped, even the little man in the white clothes Jessica had assumed was Scheherazade's trainer.

"Hey—we've lost our escort."

Matt swiveled around. "So we have. Ravi?" he called.

The man waved his stick and answered something.

"What did he say?"

"I have no idea, but I hope it was something like 'you'll be fine without me.'"

"Will we be?" Jessica had twisted so she could see behind them. When Matt turned back, his face was just inches from hers.

His eyes warmed. "We'll be more than fine."

In the few heartbeats before she turned away, awareness charged the air between them. But she did turn away, because for now, awareness was enough.

It was going to be an interesting ride.

However, it was by no means a smooth ride. Scheherazade nodded her head as she walked and her rolling gait made Jessica tense and grip the sides of the open box they sat in.

"I've got you," Matt said, his voice low.

And he did. Jessica closed her eyes and relaxed against him, lulled by the rhythmic sway and the sensation of Matt's arms around her.

"You feel a lot different than Sam did." Matt's voice was barely above a whisper.

She smiled, even though she knew he couldn't see.

JESSICA WAS IN HIS ARMS once more. It wasn't strictly necessary for him to sit with his arms around her waist, but he couldn't help himself.

He was conscious of every inch of her body that touched his, from her back to her thighs. Her skirt was bunched up around her knees and he loved looking at the contrast of her legs against the elephant's wrinkled gray skin. And then she leaned her head against him and it was all he could do to keep from burying his nose in her hair. He had to say something just to keep from pressing his lips against the top of her head. *You feel a lot different than Sam did.* How lame.

She ignored it, and he should be glad.

"How did Sam like it up here?" she asked.

"You saw. He handled it just fine. Now when he gets on Black Star, the horse will seem much smaller."

"Very clever. That was nice of you, Matt."

He was pleased by her praise. "No problem. I'm hoping he can relax some so we can go on our little roundup." Matt had planned a couple of days checking the herd and nights camping out under the stars, but until Sam was more comfortable being on a horse, he wouldn't have a good time.

"You don't have to do that. I know what I said back at Lost Springs, but I never intended for you to devote all your time to Sam."

"Except for the riding lessons, I'm not doing much extra. Just going about my business. He'll earn his keep when we fix that paddock fence, though."

A low-hanging branch was straight ahead. "One of the hazards of elephant riding," he said, and they ducked.

Matt was painfully aware that his body was covering hers, and the pain had nothing to do with tree branches. It was a sweet agony, but he didn't know how much more of this elephant ride he could take.

"You've got to be limber to ride an elephant," Jessica said, laughing when she sat back up.

Matt liked her laugh and the way she usually ended it by tucking her hair behind her ear, as though uncertain whether or not she should have laughed.

She resettled herself and he closed his eyes as she ended up even closer than before.

He bent his head and inhaled just above her neck, detecting faint traces of the perfume she'd applied that morning.

One false step from Scheherazade and his lips would touch her shoulder, or her neck, or the soft place just beneath her ear.

Matt found himself wishing for the surefooted elephant to stumble. Just once. Just once, so he'd know how her skin tasted.

"Where are we going?" she asked.

Matt leaned back before answering. "I thought I'd show you the circus animal cemetery. Some of these animals were with their human trainers for twenty years or more. After they've traveled, lived and performed together, it's like they've become a family member.''

"That sounds interesting," she said with polite enthusiasm.

He'd been fascinated the first time he'd seen the cemetery, but Jessica was used to a more exciting, sophisticated life. From some of the things she'd said, he guessed that she'd traveled a lot and had really seen the world.

He'd seen the world, too, but he didn't think an extensive tour of third-rate apartment buildings and rooming houses counted.

Jessica's world was a different world from his and he shouldn't let a few appreciative looks and the smell of her perfume make him forget. She wasn't for him. She never would be.

"I've been meaning to ask—what are those symbols nailed to the trees?"

"They're a record of the clans or performing troupes who've wintered here. And I think some have special meanings like welcome, or stay away. Some language the carny folk know, and I don't."

"It's Tom Andersen's work, isn't it?"

"Yes." He was surprised she remembered the name.

"I do want to meet him before we go back to the house. If he'll agree to it, I just know I can keep him in commissions for the next year. Outdoor ironwork is making a comeback in Wyoming."

"Old Tom will probably be glad of the work." If it paid much, Matt might take it up himself.

"And I'll be glad to have him in the Fremont catalog. Our custom work has been what's kept the company in business. We can't offer the price breaks the big companies can, but we can do the custom work that isn't profitable enough for them.''

Matt asked a few questions that kept her talking. It was easier than the silences, which made him aware of the way their bodies touched and rubbed together as the elephant continued her swaying walk.

''I probably like building houses for other people because I've never had one of my own,'' she said in response to some remark he'd made.

''What do you mean you never had a house of your own?'' That mansion she lived in was house enough for five families.

''When I was growing up, my dad traveled around the world giving lectures. We always lived in rented houses or hotels. There is an apartment in Denver, but we were never there long. It was mostly for storage and a place to give as our permanent residence. When I was thirteen, I went off to boarding school, and then I met Sam's father and moved into the Fremont house, but it isn't mine. It's really Sam's now, and someday, when he's grown, I guess I'll finally move into a place of my own.''

''Why didn't you and Sam move into a place of your own?''

''After his father died, I didn't want to. I wanted Sam to grow up in a real home, you know, with traditions and holidays and notches of how much he's grown each year cut into the door of his closet. I mean, he's in the same room his dad had as a little boy and his notches are right there next to his father's. Isn't that great?''

''Yeah,'' Matt whispered. ''Really great.''

If he'd ever fantasized that a miracle would occur and he and Jessica might end up together, her words just squashed it.

Jessica turned to look at him. "I'm sorry. I've been babbling on and on about homes and houses. I forgot that you grew up at Lost Springs."

She'd heard the bleakness in his voice and misunderstood it. He wasn't going to correct her. "I've got a home now." He made himself smile down at her, then look away.

She continued to study him and he was afraid she wouldn't drop the subject. Fortunately he saw Tom's signpost for the cemetery. "Here's our turn."

"Does Scheherazade know that?"

"Probably, but we're going to tell her to turn, anyway. Press your left foot behind her ear and say 'chi.'"

"Chi," Jessica repeated, but the elephant ignored her.

"Chi!" Jessica pressed harder, her body pressed equally hard against Matt's. "Chi! Chi!"

At the last minute, the elephant slowed and took the path toward the cemetery.

The trail wasn't as well traveled and they had to push tree branches out of their way until they came to a clearing.

"Oh, look!"

"Scheherazade, dok!" Matt leaned back, pulling Jessica with him, and the elephant lumbered to a stop.

Before them were monuments and headstones depicting bears, tigers, monkeys, dogs, horses and lions and an elephant mausoleum. The stonework was as carved and as elaborate, even more so, as in any human cemetery. Flowers bloomed around many of the graves. Iron planters held cascading baskets of ferns and ivy. Sometimes when things got tough and Matt wondered why he just didn't give up, he'd come out here and think.

"It's beautiful!"

Jessica seemed as enchanted with it as he'd been, and he was glad.

"Carmen and Katya keep it up. They each have their own group of helpers. It's an ongoing rivalry."

"Do you ever let visitors come here?"

"People come here if they know about it, I guess."

She shifted until she could see him. "I mean advertise it and give tours." She gestured around them. "You could clear more of this area and make a park for picnics. This would be a fun Sunday outing for families and it would make you a little extra money."

He'd never thought of doing so before. It might be something to bring up with Krinkov.

Jessica patted Scheherazade. "You could give elephant rides, too."

"Don't know about that. Scheherazade has paid her dues."

"Well, it was a thought."

He smiled down at her. "It's a good thought. As you know, I do need the money," he forced himself to add. "The circus people claim that old Barnaby had some payment they'd given him stashed somewhere, but I've never been able to find it. You know, on the way to Lost Springs, I saw signs for the Kingston Wildlife Sanctuary outside San Angelo and all the sponsors for it. I thought I might try finding a sponsor but I don't know how to go about it."

He wished he had Rex's smooth way of asking, but this was the best he could do. He hoped Jessica understood what he was asking. If she became his sponsor, then at least he'd have a chance of seeing her in the future someplace other than in his dreams.

"I have no idea how to get a sponsor," she replied. "I could call Lauren for you. She'd know."

"Lauren?"

"DeVane. She's a friend of mine who does that type of thing."

"Oh, yeah. That would be great." So it hadn't occurred to Jessica that she could maintain a connection with the ranch by becoming a sponsor herself. He swallowed his disappointment. It had been a long shot, anyway.

They set Scheherazade on a circular path around the cemetery, stopping frequently to admire the stonework and read the inscriptions.

Matt soaked up these moments with Jessica, knowing that they probably wouldn't be alone together like this before she left next week. When she wasn't watching, he stared at her, determined to memorize every expression she made, the way her mouth moved when she talked and the gestures she made with her hands.

They completed the circle and had reached the path that would take them out of the clearing when Jessica leaned back and shouted, "Dok!"

The elephant stopped.

"You have to say 'chi' to get her to turn back to the village."

"No, I meant stop." Jessica carefully twisted, then drew her leg over the elephant's head until she was sitting sideways, her legs draped over the sides of the seat.

"What are you doing?"

She looked first around the cemetery, then down at her clasped hands, and finally met his eyes. "When are you going to kiss me?"

His heart thudded heavily. If she only knew how much he longed to. Matt stared at the mouth only inches away from his. "I'm not."

She waited, clearly not believing him.

Matt held his breath to avoid touching her. He couldn't be strong if he touched her.

She looked away, then back again. "I thought…I got the impression that you wanted to."

He swallowed, his nerves screaming. "I do."

Her face softened. "Well, if you're waiting for a signal from me…"

"I can't." His voice was a ragged whisper.

Jessica reached up and touched his face, her caress raising gooseflesh along his arms. "Why not?"

"Because I won't want to stop." He caught her hand and flirted with fire by pressing his lips to the palm before lowering it away from his cheek. "Because I won't be able to stop."

She gave him a wry smile. "I doubt things will progress too far while we're sitting on top of an elephant."

It was after they got off the elephant that Matt was worried about. Even the *idea* of kissing her made it difficult for him to think of anything else.

At the end of next week, she was going to walk away, and if he weren't careful, she'd take his heart with her.

"Jessica, I—"

Scheherazade had reached out with her trunk to wind it around the lower branches of the tree growing at the edge of the clearing. She took a step backward to pull the leaves and threw Jessica off balance.

She lurched sideways, arms flailing. Matt grabbed for her and pulled her to him.

All his good resolutions were forgotten as he felt her in his arms once more. With insistent fingers, he tilted her chin up and then claimed her mouth with his.

He was going to hurt, anyway. Might as well know exactly what he couldn't have.

Matt intended to be tender and restrained in the sophisticated way he imagined the men she'd dated had kissed her.

He was none of those things.

There was nothing gentle about the way he clutched her to him and forced her lips apart, demanding a response from her. There was nothing restrained about the way he buried his hands in her hair and trailed kisses from her mouth to her shoulder and back again. And how could saying her name over and over again be sophisticated?

His kiss was raw and elemental, with none of the polished finesse a woman like Jessica would be accustomed to.

Matt didn't care. He loved the taste of her, the smell of her and the feel of her, and used his mouth and hands to tell her so.

The small sound she made barely registered, but the way she pulled her head back did.

"Let me go."

Horrified, Matt dropped his arms. What had he done? She must despise him, but no more than he despised himself. She was only interested in a light flirtation, not a mauling. He felt sick with self-loathing.

Jessica shifted her position so that she faced him more fully, then wound her arms around his neck. "That's better," she said, and drew his head to hers.

Surprise and relief kept him immobile.

Jessica Fremont was kissing him.

And doing a darn good job.

Her tongue met his thrust for thrust. Her arms held him close to her as tightly as he held her.

"Matthew," she breathed, using his whole name the way the others did.

He'd started a fire within himself that threatened to consume him. The blood pounded in his ears and his senses were filled with her. He pulled back to drag in much-needed air and Jessica kissed his chin and his jaw, then his neck.

He heard a pop and then more as she unsnapped his shirt.

Splaying her hands over his torso, she reached around him, then kissed his throat and chest, her blond hair a stark contrast against the darkness of his.

He shivered with wanting. "Jessica," he gasped, trying to tell her what she was doing to him.

"You're so strong and you make me feel so safe," she murmured, working her way back up to his shoulder.

She wasn't safe, not the way he was feeling.

He wanted to take her to his bed, make love to her and wake up in the morning with her by his side. He wanted to know that she'd be there the next morning, and the next.

He never wanted to let her go.

And that's when he knew he must.

CHAPTER TWELVE

KISSING MATT was absolutely the best idea she'd ever had.

There had been enough pent-up electricity between them to light up the entire state of Texas, and frankly, it was long past time a man flipped a few of her switches.

Jessica had expected an initial awkwardness and a few false starts before she got back into the swing of things. She had *not* expected a full-out sensual assault— or the intensity of her response.

Matt kissed her the way he looked at her—as though she were the only woman in the world for him. He even had Jessica believing it herself, so she was shocked when he trapped her wandering hands, held them against his bare chest and said, "We have to stop."

"What?" Shouldn't that have been her line?

For a moment, the only sounds were those of their hard breathing and Scheherazade munching on grass.

Matt kissed her hands and gently, but insistently, held them away. "We both know you're leaving next week."

"That's next week."

"Jessica…"

"I understand," she assured him quickly. "No strings. No promises."

He looked pained. Slowly he began fastening his

shirt. "That's just it. I'm not the kind of guy who goes in for flings, and knowing that you're going to be leaving, well…"

She blinked. "You're making me sound like…a woman of loose morals," she finished, trying for a laugh. She managed a shaky one.

"No, no." He cupped her jaw, the way she'd cupped his earlier. "It's me. I…all the people I was close to in my life left me. My counselor at Lost Springs warned me that it would be hard for me to make friends and have relationships. I've been hurt so many times that—"

"Oh, Matt!" She felt horrible. No wonder he'd held back when another man would have already made a move on her.

"But even knowing about it, it still takes me a long time to get close to someone." He gazed at her, then said simply, "And when I do, I want her to be around for a while."

But she was leaving. There was nothing she could say to the contrary. Nodding, she twisted around and positioned her feet behind the elephant's ears. "We'd better get back," she said, trying to make her voice sound normal. "I want to meet Tom Andersen and you have to talk to Krinkov about the vet."

BY UNSPOKEN MUTUAL agreement, Matt and Jessica avoided being alone with each other. And, with everything going on around the ranch, it was easy to avoid each other, period.

That didn't mean Jessica didn't think about him pretty much all the time, though.

Their kiss on the elephant had given her a lot to think about. She'd realized that her "fling" days were long past. And if Matt wasn't fling material, then that meant he was something she wasn't ready to acknowledge.

The vet came the next day, even though Krinkov grumbled mightily. Matt drove the doctor to the village to check on the other circus animals after he treated Sheba.

Sam reported that Sheba had really big pills she had to swallow and they had to hide them in her food.

But Sheba didn't want to eat food. Jessica sent Lita to buy the most tender steaks she could. She also got rolls of pennies for Caesar, who was miffed at all the attention being given to the tiger and not to him. He and Sam spent hours playing the coin game.

While Matt was busy with the vet, Jessica started directing the repairs to the barn. The retired canvas men barely acknowledged her presence, even though Frank pretended to consult with and defer to her. That was all right with Jessica. At least it gave her an excuse to stay out of Matt's way.

They did have one lengthy discussion when Matt returned from driving the vet back to his helicopter.

It was at the end of the day, and Jessica and Frank were at the shed, discussing how best to go about rebuilding it. Frank wanted to salvage as much of the old one as he could for the village, and Jessica was trying to persuade him that the metal was so rusty, it would disintegrate if they attempted to move it.

Matt drove his truck into the ranch yard and headed their way. "What's all this?" he said even before he'd slammed the door shut.

"Frank wants salvage rights on the old shed," Jessica told him. "But structurally, it wouldn't be safe."

"No—I meant *this*." He pointed to the pile of metal siding.

"That will be the new shed."

Matt stared at it, then at her. "What new shed?"

Jessica stared back. "The new shed to replace *that*." She pointed to the rusting building.

"I believe it is now that I should busy myself at the barn." Frank started backing away. "Perhaps to pay a sick call on Sheba. Perhaps to check and see if those lazy canvas men have finished the repairs and have started on the fence. It doesn't matter. I will be at the barn." He limped away quickly.

Matt crossed his arms. Jessica ignored the way his shirt pulled against his shoulders. "I don't recall ordering materials for a new shed."

"I ordered them."

"Why?"

"Why?" She gestured to the old building. "A strong wind and that thing's gone. At the least, it leaks."

"I know it does, but there are things around here that need fixing sooner than that shed."

"I ordered fencing for you, too."

"I'm talking about the bunkhouse. I realize it's only got folks living in it during the winter, but I'd at least like to keep it dry and warm inside."

"We can fix the bunkhouse. Why didn't you say something?"

"Because I can't afford to!"

"But *I'm* paying!"

"Did it ever occur to you that I might want to use that money of yours for other things—things like feeding animals?"

It hadn't occurred to her. "I'll make up for the cost of the shed." And probably the appliances, too. He didn't know about those, but she knew better than to bring them up now.

"No."

"Come on, Matt. I don't want some animal starving because you have a new shed."

"I said no. Just don't go ordering anything else without checking with me first." With an abrupt nod, he spun on his heel and strode into the ranch house.

It had been a stupid argument, Jessica told herself. They weren't really arguing about sheds, they were trying to keep an emotional distance between them.

It wasn't working.

She'd noticed the way he'd looked at her. She'd probably looked at him the same way.

But not acknowledging their feelings was for the best.

"Mom!" A dusty Sam came running into the kitchen the next morning.

Lita and Jessica were having their usual gingersnap break.

"Me and Matt's gonna go on a roundup!"

"Matt and I," she corrected. Rachel was going to have a fit when they got back and she heard how Sam's grammar had deteriorated.

"He sent me in here to pack!"

Jessica stood. "When are you leaving?"

"As soon as I get ready," Sam said, and ran off to his room.

The door quietly opened and closed behind her. Jessica turned to find Matt standing in the doorway. He looked tired, as though he hadn't been sleeping well.

"Boy'll need a bedroll," Lita mumbled, and headed out of the kitchen.

Why was it people kept leaving the two of them alone?

As always, Matt's eyes were on her.

"I thought you weren't taking Sam out until the end of the week," she said.

Matt walked over to the kitchen sink, his boots loud in the silence. "Changed my mind."

The strained situation between them had something to do with it, no doubt. "Look, I've apologized for ordering supplies without telling you. I didn't think you were the type of man to carry a grudge."

Matt turned off the water and grabbed a towel. "I'm not mad at you, Jessica." He half smiled. "I'm just finding it difficult to be around you and not touch you."

Then touch me. She couldn't believe she'd found the one man in the universe who wanted to protect her from herself.

He scorched her with a look, then turned and hung up the towel. "I thought it best to put some distance between us."

What, did he think she was going to throw herself at him? He'd been more than plain about not wanting a short-term affair.

And, Jessica admitted, not particularly proud of herself, she would have been using him to test herself. In a few days, they'd be gone from here, and there was emotional safety in knowing that. She didn't have to become involved with him on any level except purely physical.

Matt must have sensed that, darn it.

She changed the subject. "How is Sam doing with the horse? Is he ready for this?"

Matt nodded. "The elephant ride did the trick. He isn't intimidated by Black Star anymore."

At the mention of the elephant ride, there was another awkward silence between them.

"I'll go help Sam," Jessica said. As she left the kitchen, she could feel Matt's gaze on her.

MATT AND SAM WERE GONE for three days. It was all Jessica could do to keep from hopping in her car and driving around until she saw that they were all right.

There was one welcome distraction: the new appliances arrived and required a state visit from Carmen and Katya. Lita made a great big German-chocolate cake for the occasion.

This time, after Jessica drank her tea, she automatically swished it around three times and turned it in the saucer before handing it to Carmen.

Carmen beamed, then bent to read the leaves. Even Katya seemed interested in what her rival saw in the cup.

"Does the letter *r* mean anyone to you?" Carmen asked.

"My mother-in-law is named Rachel," Jessica answered, thinking she must have mentioned it earlier. "Why do you ask?"

Carmen shrugged. "I see three *r*'s in the cup. Two near the rim, one of those is also near the handle. I see dots indicating a journey in the near future."

"Well, I'm supposed to leave this week," Jessica pointed out.

"Not you," Carmen said. "Her."

It was wild conjecture. It meant nothing.

"Lovely Jessica," Frank called, interrupting them. He opened the kitchen door. Seeing his wife, he smiled. "And my equally lovely darling." Limping over, he gave her a huge kiss.

"She claims to see the future, yet she does not see through him," Katya said in an aside.

But Jessica felt Carmen and Frank were genuinely fond of each other.

Frank cleared his throat. ''Jessica, Sheba—she doesn't look so good. I found these.''

He held out his hand. In it were three huge capsules that the tiger had obviously discovered in her food and refused to eat.

''Oh dear. Where is she?''

''Under the tree.''

Followed by the others, Jessica jogged out to the old pecan tree. Sheba lay in about the same spot that her triumph over the snake had taken place. Her ribs showed and each breath was a wheeze. Caesar sat beside her head, grooming her and making eerily mournful sounds.

Jessica absently reached into her pocket. ''Coin.''

Caesar gave a subdued chirp and went back to grooming Sheba.

''Yeah, you're right. How can I think of playing a game at a time like this.'' She returned the penny to her pocket and squatted down to look at the tiger.

Carmen, Frank and Katya arrived and stood silently.

''Do you think she's in pain?'' Jessica asked.

''If she is, she bears it well,'' Frank said.

''She was always one of the most reliable performers,'' his wife added. ''If Gordo took an animal out to show, Sheba was the one he took. She'd always draw a good tip.''

Katya nodded. ''And if one of those young hooligans in the crowd teased her, she never snapped. Gordo always gave her a treat for resisting.''

Jessica wished they'd stop talking as though the tiger were gone. ''Maybe we should call the vet.''

No one said anything.

She looked up in time to see them exchanging uncertain looks.

"Don't know if you should, lady." Reminding Jessica of Scheherazade, Frank laboriously got down on one knee and ran his hand over the tiger.

Sheba rumbled.

Jessica couldn't stand it. "I want to call the vet. Do you know which vet Matt uses, Frank?"

"He comes for a price."

"Don't worry about that. What's his name?"

Frank seemed hesitant and glanced up at the women standing behind Jessica. "Dr. Harrelson. Martin Harrelson. He lives in Kerrville."

Wherever that was. "Thanks, Frank." The doctor's number was probably in the leather address book Matt kept on the ranch office desk.

Jessica rubbed the old tiger's head. "Hang in there, girl. We'll get you fixed up."

The doctor couldn't come until the next day. Throughout the morning, Jessica tried without luck to coax Sheba to eat. She would barely drink.

At last, Jessica saw the helicopter fly overhead and land in the flat pasture just on this side of the ravine. Frank drove out to get the vet.

Dr. Harrelson was a youngish, bespectacled man, with long pale fingers and an obvious rapport with his patients.

"I was surprised to get the call," he told Jessica as he knelt next to Sheba, who was still under the tree.

From above them, Caesar chattered.

"Hey, Caesar. How's it going?" The doctor held his hand next to the tiger's nose, then stroked her before getting out his stethoscope.

"Sheba wasn't taking her medicine and now she won't eat at all," Jessica said.

"Those were pain pills. Matt and I decided to just make her comfortable."

"What do you mean?" Jessica asked with dread.

"She's got tummy troubles, don't you, old girl?" The vet got a metal box out of his knapsack and unlocked it with a key. "I don't know for certain, could be her liver, could be a number of things. Without operating, I can't tell. Basically, she's just old."

"Why don't you operate?"

"Cost, for one thing. Transportation—"

"I'll pay."

Dr. Harrelson looked at her, then took a vial of amber liquid from the box and filled a syringe with it. "Just because you can doesn't mean you should. This will make sure she doesn't feel any pain for a while," he said, and injected the medicine in Sheba's shoulder.

Within moments, the tiger's eyes closed and her breathing changed.

"What about when she wakes up?" Jessica asked.

"I'll leave a vial and some syringes with Matt. He knows how to administer them." Dr. Harrelson gave her a long look. "I could euthanize her right now while she's asleep. She'll never know."

"No!" Horrified, Jessica rocked back on her heels. "If you won't do the operation to help this animal, then at least leave the syringes."

"Your call." Dr. Harrelson made some notes on a pad, then tore the sheet off and handed it to Jessica along with two vials and a handful of syringes. "But I don't think you'll need them all," he said ominously. "Any other patients for me to see today?"

"Not that I know of."

"You sure? I don't usually come this far for one animal."

"I owe her." Jessica told him the snake story, but he didn't seem impressed.

"Okay, then." He rummaged in his knapsack and took out a billing notebook. Checking his watch, he wrote several figures in a column, looked skyward for a moment, scribbled some more, then tore off the page and handed it to Jessica.

"Would you give that to Matt for me?" Squatting, he began repacking his knapsack.

Jessica looked at the total. Wasn't there a decimal point missing?

The helicopter was by far the largest expense, but the amount of the bill was enough to make even Jessica blink. "I'd rather pay for this myself. Will you take an out-of-town check?"

MATT AND SAM ARRIVED BACK two afternoons later. Jessica had spent the morning photographing Tom Andersen's work for the catalog. In addition to the ironworker, she'd found a wood carver and was well pleased with her new additions to the catalog.

The best news was that after her sleep, Sheba had awakened and actually ate for the first time in several days.

Jessica was working on her laptop in the ranch office when she saw Matt and Sam come riding in. Mindful of Matt's advice, she didn't immediately run screaming from the house shouting, "My baby!" the way she wanted to.

Instead she watched them—both of them—as they rode toward the newly repaired barn.

Sam looked exhausted, she thought. And filthy. He

was wearing the same clothes as when he left. Maybe she should go outside and greet them—and hose them down.

But she didn't. Instead she stayed in the ranch office, pretending that she didn't know they were back, while they spent an interminable amount of time in the barn.

At last, she saw Sam come running from the barn. Halfway, he had to stop and walk, and even then, he veered toward the tree where Sheba and Caesar were before coming inside to see her, his mother.

"Mom! We're back, and I'm starved!"

Now Jessica let herself go greet him.

Lita was fussing about him getting the floor dirty, but she'd given him a glass of milk and a leftover cinnamon bun wrapped in a napkin by the time Jessica made it to the kitchen.

Regardless of how dirty he was, Jessica gave him a big hug.

"Mom, it was so cool out there. Me and Matt found a sick cow and we helped her. Then we counted the herd. And we rode all day long and I got sore. Then we camped and built a fire and I burned my hand." He held it up, but moved it before Jessica could examine his injury.

"Let me see."

"That's nothing. I got others worse."

He continued babbling as he drank milk and stuffed wads of Lita's cinnamon roll into his mouth. "And Matt even let me drink coffee. Cowboys drink coffee, you know."

Matt, who'd obviously taken the time to wash his face and hands before coming inside, arrived at the screen door in time to hear Sam's coffee announcement.

Jessica raised an eyebrow at him and he grinned, dark

eyes flashing. She smiled back, deciding to overlook him giving her son caffeine this time.

Matt sniffed the air. "Something sure smells good. What're you cooking, Lita?"

"Cornish game hens and wild rice with mushrooms," Lita answered. She'd really taken to the concept of ordering food through the mail.

Matt stared at her, his expression comical.

"What did she say?" Sam asked.

"Midget chickens and black rice," Jessica told him.

"I like those," Sam said.

"Well, if you want to eat any, then you'll have to go take a—"

"Hey."

Matt was looking around the kitchen at the new refrigerator, dishwasher and stove. "What's all this?"

"The old stove done quit, and your lady bought all new."

Matt shot Jessica a look, considerably less warm than the one he'd given her earlier.

"I ordered them when I ordered the building materials," she explained. "A gift."

"You should have told me."

She probably should have. "I wanted it to be a surprise."

"It is," he said, and the tone of his voice left no doubt that it was not a pleasant one.

"Sam, go ahead and get started with your bath. I'll be in to help you in a minute."

"Mom! I can take a bath by myself," he said disgustedly.

"And how would I know? You obviously haven't had one since you've been gone."

"Aw, Mom." Sam set his empty glass on the table and trudged off to the bathroom.

Lita was ignoring, or was unaware of, the tension between Matt and Jessica. She demonstrated all the facets of the new kitchen appliances until Matt excused himself to wash up before dinner.

Then she came over and squeezed Jessica's shoulder. "Don't you worry none, Jessie. He'll be right and tight after he sets his spoon to my chocolate mousse."

An exhausted Sam couldn't stay awake long enough for the chocolate mousse.

Jessica took him off to bed, relishing the opportunity to tuck him in. She had a feeling these times were nearing an end.

Sam continued to talk as she pulled the covers up to his chin, telling her all the adventures he'd had with Matt. Just before he fell asleep, he murmured, "Do we have to go home?"

"You know we do. What would Gramma think if we never came home?"

Even near sleep, Sam frowned. "I like it here. I don't like living with Gramma."

Jessica stroked the hair back from his forehead. "What about all your friends?"

"I have new friends here. Let's stay, please, Mom?"

She should drop it and let him get to sleep. "There's a lot of hard work to be done on a ranch."

"I know." He yawned and pulled his hand from under the covers. "See? I've done work." His palm had a blister on it. "'Night, Mom."

Jessica kissed his temple and left the room.

She should have expected this reaction, yet she was still troubled. In spite of the blister, was Matt showing Sam only the fun parts of being a cowboy on a ranch?

Although she'd hoped Sam would enjoy the cowboy life for a few days, she'd never imagined he would take to it as he had. Maybe she should say something to Matt. Sam should see the downside to ranching, as well.

Lita had stayed and eaten with them—mainly so she could load the dishwasher, Jessica suspected as she came in the door after checking on Sheba.

The housekeeper was getting ready to leave for the night. "I put another pan of cinnamon rolls in the refrigerator," she said. "You just let 'em sit out on the counter tomorrow morning until they get big, then bake 'em in the oven."

"Thanks, Lita. Have you seen Matt?"

"He's gone into the office."

Jessica nodded.

Lita took her purse from the peg behind the pantry door. "Now, you stand your ground about the new stove and such. It was high time we had new here and a woman needs working tools as much as any man, but they don't see it that way."

Lita made a good point. Jessica smiled. "Okay."

She couldn't figure out why Matt would be angry. The cost of the appliances was coming from her money, so he shouldn't care. Maybe it was more that she'd done something without his knowledge than any real objection.

He was going through the mail when she found him, slicing through the envelopes with a mother-of-pearl-handled knife.

"I wanted to thank you for giving Sam the time of his life," she said.

"My pleasure." He opened an envelope and plucked out a sheet of paper.

After glancing at it, he added it to the growing stack

on his left, then attacked another envelope with unnecessary vigor, Jessica thought.

Might as well get on with it. "I apologize if you're angry about the new appliances. But the stove wasn't working and the rest of them were equally ancient."

"I know how old they were."

"Lita was cooking half the stuff at her place, anyway."

He gave her a brief look. "Since she's usually only cooking for me, it worked out okay."

"The refrigerator was not running efficiently. The new one will save you money in the long run because it uses less electricity."

"It looks twice as big."

It probably was, she had to concede. "Well, it won't use any *more* electricity than the old one. And it has an ice maker."

He grabbed another envelope. "Did it occur to you that I might want to spend money on something other than an ice maker?"

"I'm sorry," she apologized again. "I told you they were a gift."

"I don't need your gifts." He unfolded the letter and stared at it.

His pride was hurt. She understood. "I was able to use the Fremont Construction account to get them wholesale for—"

"What the—" Matt stared at the paper, then at Jessica. "This is an account summary from the vet." He pointed to the payments column. "According to this, he was out here a couple of days ago. Is that true?"

She should have known that if he begrudged the new appliances, he'd have a fit over her paying the vet bill.

"Sheba wasn't eating and I couldn't reach you, so I called him."

"And Frank let you?"

"He wasn't wildly enthusiastic about it, but he didn't stop me."

"He should have," Matt told her bluntly.

Jessica was trying very hard to be reasonable and see Matt's side. "I'll admit that I was surprised at how much it cost. However, I paid—"

"I'm aware that you paid. And are you aware that between the vet visits—both of them—the kitchen stuff, the wood and the new shed that almost all the money you're paying to let your son play cowboy has been spent?"

And this was her thanks for trying to do something nice for somebody? "I said I'd pay for the new appliances and I've already paid for the second vet visit. But wait. Why don't I pay for the building materials, too? I'll just go get my checkbook and write you a check for five thousand dollars that you can spend any way you want."

"Typical. You think all problems can be solved by throwing money at them."

Jessica had started for the door, but at that, she wheeled back around. "Wrong. I deal with *money* problems by throwing money at them. Money is just a tool. I use it, but I know what it can do and what it can't do."

He looked at her with an unreadable expression. "Sorry. I was out of line." Slitting open another envelope, he barely glanced at the contents before adding them to the stack.

From where she stood, Jessica could see Past Due stamped across the top of the pink paper.

Stubborn man.

"Was there anything else you needed?" He didn't look at her as he spoke. "If not, I've got some paperwork I need to catch up on."

Jessica hated the strain between them. "Actually I did come in here to discuss something with you—Sam."

"What about him?"

"He's having a wonderful time. Maybe too wonderful."

Matt tossed the knife on the desk and swiveled in the leather chair. "What do you mean?"

"He told me he doesn't want to go home."

A corner of Matt's mouth tilted upward. "That'll pass."

"I think so, too, but I'd appreciate it if you wouldn't glamorize ranch life for him."

"*Glamorize* it?" Matt gave a crack of laughter.

"Yes! This place is like a little boy's fantasy. There are circus animals wandering around, he gets to ride a horse, go camping, ride an *elephant,* learn card tricks—why would he want to leave?"

"If anyone has glamorized it, you have. First off, Sam would have had to watch me sell my horse. I still may. And next, I either would have fixed the broken stove or eaten cold food." He dug in the pile and waved the vet's bill at her. "If you and Sam hadn't been here—if I hadn't had the money you brought—I never would have called the vet. Sam would have had a real hard lesson in the value of animals. There isn't room on a ranch for sentiment. Sheba's old and she doesn't contribute. There's no way to justify this expense for her. That money would have bought a lot of feed."

"There are lots of animals around here who don't contribute."

Matt's anger faded. "You got that right. And it's going to bankrupt me. When Sam and I were out, I could see that the grazing land isn't going to produce enough to last through the winter. I'll have to cut my herd—again." Elbows on the desktop, he rubbed his forehead with both hands.

A door to Jessica's heart opened, a door she'd kept locked since Sam's father died.

This was the wrong time, the wrong place and with the wrong man, but she couldn't help it. For the second time in her life, love had struck quickly and completely.

Matt exhaled. "I'm going to lose this place, Jessica. I'm going to lose my home."

"Oh, Matt." To a man who'd grown up without one, a home was everything. "I'm so sorry." She hesitated, then touched his shoulder. She wanted to do more. Much more.

"And the worst of it is that all those people and animals will lose their homes, too."

Jessica knelt by the chair so she could see his eyes. "It doesn't have to be that way. Let me help."

He looked at her, his expression as vulnerable as she'd ever seen it. Reaching out, he cupped the side of her head, caressing her cheek with his thumb. "You've already helped plenty."

Jessica leaned into his touch before standing abruptly. "I'm going to get my checkbook and you're going to figure out exactly how much you need to fix this place up and make it profitable again."

"Jessica, wait."

But this time, she wasn't turning back. She couldn't stand seeing Matt so dejected. He was a good man. A fine, honest, dependable man. A caring man. A strong man whose openhearted kisses had touched her in a way she never thought she could be touched again.

A man she loved.

CHAPTER THIRTEEN

JESSICA REACHED HER bedroom. Her leather purse was on the nightstand and she quickly walked toward it, ignoring Matt's footsteps behind her.

"Jessica, will you stop throwing your money around? This isn't your problem."

"Why won't you let me help you?" She dug in her purse for her checkbook.

"I'm not taking your money," he stated flatly.

"Why are we arguing about this again? You need it. I've got it." She found her checkbook, turned and took a step forward at the same moment Matt did.

She ran into the solid wall of his chest. He reached out to steady her and their gazes locked.

His eyes were dark with pain, frustration and a hungry desire.

They stood there long enough for Jessica to become aware of the ticking of the old china clown clock on the bedside table.

Still, it was a short time, considering how everything changed between them.

"Jessica." Matt said her name on a sigh of surrender. Taking the checkbook from her nerveless fingers, he tossed it on the table. "I don't need your money as much as I need you," he whispered, and pulled her to him.

Jessica fell into his arms willingly. All their arguing,

all their disagreements had only been ways to deny their feelings.

When her lips met his, Jessica forgot why denying their feelings was supposed to be such a great idea.

She'd spent all week telling herself she only wanted a getting-back-into-circulation fling with this man. And if Matt hadn't been the man he was, that might have been all she had. As it was, time and distance had allowed her feelings to deepen, though until a few moments ago, she hadn't been aware of it.

Matt kissed her the way he looked at her—with total and complete attention. She had no doubt that he was thinking of her and only her. He wasn't worrying about the future, or if there would be a future.

There was only now.

As he held her, kissing her with a desperate hunger, she felt a shifting inside her. A realignment. A freeing.

And a recognition that she was being given the opportunity to love again.

That was what she was going to concentrate on now, on her feelings for Matt and his for her, without regard to timetables and circumstances, complications and... more complications.

"I tried to stay away," Matt said against her mouth.

"You're very wise. Wiser than you know."

Using both hands to frame her face, he dragged his mouth away and pressed his forehead against hers. "Tell me to stop and I will, but tell me now."

"Stop now and you and your steers will have a lot in common."

She felt his smile. "Not a chance, honey." He nuzzled the side of her neck, sending delightful tingles up and down her spine.

"Which brings to mind something else..."

"Mmm?" His nuzzles were more insistent.

"I don't want you to get the wrong idea…" *Oh, honestly, be a big girl about this, Jessica.* "My friend Liz gave me a going away present. It's in my purse—the purse on the nightstand. Right behind us. So when we need—"

He interrupted her with a lengthy kiss. "Frank gave me the same present after our elephant ride."

Jessica smiled and looped her arms around his neck. "Don't we have thoughtful friends?"

He smiled, kissed her quickly and said, "Hang on. I've always wanted to do this."

Bending down, he scooped her into his arms and carried her to the bed, then set her gently on it.

Jessica sighed. "That was lovely. So romantic, so gentlemanly, so courtly…" So slow. She sighed again, then arched her eyebrow. "You know what *I've* always wanted to do?"

Smiling, he shook his head.

Jessica crooked her finger at him.

Matt leaned over. She grabbed the edges of his shirt and ripped it apart. "Love those snaps." She ran her hands over his chest and pushed the shirt off his shoulders. "You have beautiful shoulders. That was one of the first things I noticed about you. I thought they were broad enough to give a boy a piggyback ride."

Matt shrugged his shirt off and tossed it at the chair in the corner. He sat next to her. "I first noticed your strength."

Jessica ran a finger over the muscles in his arm. "So my workouts have paid off."

"Not that kind of strength."

The expression on her face must have reflected her puzzlement. "I know it's not the first thing a man generally looks for in a woman, and you do have plenty of the other kind, but, yes, I have to say that my first impression of you was that you were a strong woman. I liked that.''

Jessica liked the idea of being strong, too. "Come here." She patted the spot next to her.

Matt shook his head. "Well, now, ma'am, even a cowboy knows better than to come to a lady's bed wearing his boots.''

Jessica propped herself on an elbow, prepared to volunteer to help, but was fascinated by watching the muscles work in his back as he struggled to get his boots off. She sat up and ran her hands over his back and shoulders as he tugged off first one, then the other of his boots. When he finished, he carefully paired them and set them toes inward at the foot of her bed.

"Is that some kind of statement?" she asked.

"It means I plan to stay awhile."

"Good." She opened her arms.

Matt knelt over her, laced his fingers through hers and just looked at her.

First, he looked into her eyes, his own unblinking and dark. But the longer Jessica gazed back at him, the more she saw and the closer to him she felt. She saw a deep and ancient hurt that shadowed everything and knew it was his childhood.

But she saw newer emotions, too. Trust, tenderness and a growing desire.

He was looking for a specific response from her, she guessed, and was content to wait until he found it.

His gaze roamed over her face with such intensity she could almost feel it, could anticipate his touch. She shivered.

"Cold?"

She shook her head, though she wouldn't mind feeling his warm body next to hers.

His thumbs rubbed the sides of her fingers. His eyes held hers, reassuring and patient.

And Jessica relaxed. She stopped anticipating, stopped waiting for his kiss. She simply savored this time with him, knowing that this man already held a special place in her heart. She didn't question how it came to be, she only knew that it was.

Matt gave her a slow smile, then lowered his mouth to hers in a kiss that branded her soul.

When he looked at her again, Jessica understood. He was going to make *love* to her and he wanted her to realize it.

"Oh, Matt." Her eyes stung. She wasn't going to cry, was she? She didn't want him to think she was upset. "Kiss me again."

"You could kiss me," he murmured.

"I can't reach you!"

Smiling, he slowly unlaced their fingers and lowered himself beside her.

Her heart was beating so fast and all she could think about was his touch, but Jessica made herself straddle him and relaced their fingers. Then she looked at him, telling him without words of *her* past hurt and her deepened feelings for him.

She felt nervous and vulnerable and incredibly close to him. In his gaze she saw understanding—and love. She lowered her mouth to his.

The kiss was better for having waited, but Jessica sensed the waiting had ended. And about time, too. She met his tongue with an insistent thrust of hers, then gently pulled on his lower lip.

"Jessica," Matt breathed.

He grasped the edge of her T-shirt, untucking it from her skirt, then splayed his fingers against her back, warming her skin.

She sat up and returned the favor, running her hands from his rib cage over his torso, across his well-muscled chest and shoulders.

He closed his eyes. "Jessica..." He was breathing harder now, she noticed with feminine satisfaction. Lowering her head, she let her hair brush across his skin as she kissed her way down his torso.

"Jessica!" It was more of a gasp than a breath.

Grabbing her shoulders, Matt held her away from him, then undressed her, making the simple T-shirt and denim skirt seem like exotic clothing.

"Ah, the blue," he said when he saw her underwear.

"What do you mean, 'Ah, the blue'?"

He grinned. "I saw your underwear hanging on the clothesline. Every morning, I've been trying to guess which set you're wearing. I like the white ones. There didn't seem to be much to them. But the blue looked like it would be easier to take off."

"Well, here's your chance to find out."

Matt had already reached around her back. A second later he'd tossed her bra aside. "You're so beautiful," he breathed, and just gazed at her.

While he was distracted, Jessica unbuckled his jeans.

Funny thing. After that point, there was a lot less looking and a lot more action.

The first thing she did was to press her naked body fully against his, reveling in the feel of masculine strength.

"I've missed this," she whispered. "There hasn't been anyone since..."

"We'll go slow," Matt assured her.

Jessica raised her head. "Not *too* slow, I hope."

Matt gave her fiercely tender look. "Jessica, I..." He swallowed and she suspected he'd been going to say something else. "I want this to be good for you."

She touched his face. "It already is."

Matt made love to her with complete intensity, as though she were the only woman in the world. He was tender, playful, sensuous and, to her delighted surprise, passionately vocal.

With his mouth and hands, he lavished attention on every inch of her, reawakening a long-slumbering desire.

With his caring touch, he revived pieces of Jessica's heart that she'd thought were dead forever. It was a joyful lovemaking for her and she wanted to share some of that joy with him.

Wrapping her leg around him, she surprised him by rolling him over on his back, then looking at him the way he'd looked at her.

"*You're* beautiful," she said.

"I'm glad."

It was such a sweet response that she rewarded him with a trail of kisses that left him gasping.

One second she was in control, and the next her back was against the pillows.

"Jessica..."

"Where did you learn that maneuver? Roping calves?"

He didn't smile. "*Jessica.*" His voice was rough with longing.

She understood. He needed her. Now. Wrapping her arms around him, she drew him to her.

"I—"

"Hush. I want it, too."

Even so, she gasped when he entered her all at once. He gazed down at her. "Did I hurt you?"

"No," she reassured him. "It's just been such a long time."

He lay with her, allowing her to get used to his body before beginning a slow rocking that quickly built in intensity until it carried them both into a world of pleasure that healed their bruised hearts.

MATT LOOKED DOWN at a sleeping Jessica and made himself a promise: he'd be thankful for whatever time she had to give him. And he'd no longer try to stop himself from falling in love with her.

It was too late, anyway, he acknowledged, and brushed a lock of hair off her cheek. It had been too late probably from the moment she'd dragged Sam out from under his arm the first time they met.

He was going to have to leave her bed soon. Neither of them wanted to make explanations to Sam, or Lita, for that matter.

He kissed her temple. She stirred, and to his surprise, opened her eyes.

"Hi," she said softly.

"I didn't mean to wake you."

She gave him a sleepy smile. "I'm glad you did." She ran her hands over his chest and kissed his shoulder.

Something as simple as that caused his banked desire to flame with new life. Matt leaned over her, gently cupping her breast, savoring the intimacy. It would be hell when she left, but he intended to make it heaven until then.

JESSICA AWOKE EARLY the next morning feeling more alive than she had in years.

She could never go back to being the sort of person she'd been before she'd met Matt. She'd been alive, but she'd hadn't really been *living*. Sam had been everything to her, and that was an awful lot of responsibility for a boy.

No matter what happened, or didn't happen, between her and Matt, she wouldn't make the mistake of depending solely on Sam for fulfillment again.

She already had the coffee made and Lita's rolls baking when a sleepy Sam hobbled into the kitchen.

"I'm sore," he announced. "My bu—"

"Too much information," Jessica said, trying to hide her smile.

"Matt said I'd be sore and, man, is he right." Sam yawned. "I need to go feed the animals. That's my job now. Matt says I'm a real help." He rubbed his eyes then looked at Jessica. "Can't we stay longer? Please?"

Was she a horrible mother if she used that as an excuse to have extra time with Matt?

As if her thoughts had summoned him, he appeared in the doorway. It had only been hours since she'd fallen asleep in his arms, completely sated, yet if Sam weren't here, she'd be heading for the bedroom right now.

"I'm trying to get Mom to let us stay longer. You don't mind, do you, Matt?" Sam pleaded.

Matt looked at Jessica. "You're welcome to stay as long as you like."

How could she leave when she'd just found him?

"I guess we could stay another week." She looked at Matt as she spoke.

Matt's eyes darkened and Jessica caught her breath.

"Aw right!" Sam slapped Matt's hands and scampered out the door, his soreness forgotten.

She glanced back at Matt, wondering what he'd say to her.

He said nothing. In two strides, he was across the kitchen and had her in his arms, where he kissed her thoroughly and completely.

"Hold that thought until tonight," he said when he released her.

Jessica grinned. "What if I need to be reminded during the day?"

"Matt, hurry up!" they heard Sam call.

Matt gave her a wry smile. "Guess I'll have to send you a memo."

KNOWING SHE WAS BEING cowardly, Jessica had sent Rachel an E-mail about their delayed return. She would have phoned if Rachel had acknowledged any of her other messages. From remarks some of the Fremont staff she'd talked to had made, Jessica knew Rachel had read them.

She was just being stubborn.

It was the only thing marring the perfect days that followed. It wasn't often that a person had an absolutely perfect day, not to mention perfect night, and Jessica was treated to a string of them.

She abandoned her laptop and joined Matt and Sam outdoors, even riding around the newly repaired paddock on Black Star. Jessica took her turn at chores, too, ruining her nails, but who cared?

Across the ravine, they repaired the circus animals' fence, then got to help give Scheherazade a bath using Murphy's Oil Soap.

After those perfect days, Jessica was even beginning to think that she could spend the rest of her life here. These weeks had changed her. She wasn't the willful girl who'd married Sam's father, and she was no longer the overly staid young matron she'd become as his widow. She was finally a mixture of the two and she owed it all to Matt.

Matt. As a lover, he made her toes curl. Each night they spent together, they made love as though they had endless nights to do so. Neither mentioned what would happen at the end of the week.

And when he was with her son, Jessica caught herself watching them with a lump in her throat. Sam clearly adored Matt and she knew it wasn't completely one-sided. There were times when she watched them from inside the house, times she saw Matt drape an arm around her son, tousle his hair or start a water fight at the spigot that left them both soaked and laughing.

She didn't want to take Sam away from all that and, frankly, she wasn't ready to leave, either. She'd actually decided to stay on longer, when a visitor arrived at the ranch.

Rachel.

MATT COULD FORGET everything when he was in Jessica's arms, except the fact that she was leaving.

That was something he refused to think about, concentrating instead on making every moment they had alone together count. Doing so had put him behind, which was why he found himself at the computer on a hot, sunny afternoon, instead of outside with Sam and Jessica.

The mere thought of her caused an ache. He loved her and he wanted to tell her so. Last night, in an effort to keep from blurting out the words, he'd bitten his tongue so hard it had drawn blood.

She didn't love him, he knew. She couldn't. What did he have to offer her?

Everyone and everything in his life needed him, except Jessica. She was strong, independent—and there was always the money. The fact that she treated it so casually told him that she'd grown up with it and had never been caught with an empty wallet and too many days left in the month.

But Sam needed him, Matt knew. Sam needed a father. Matt would be honored to fill the role. He understood the boy and what would be good for him, because, to his surprise, Sam reminded him a lot of himself. Being with Sam was almost like getting a chance to put things right in his own life.

If he tried, he might be able to convince Jessica to stay for Sam's sake, but would Matt want her on those terms?

He turned the chair around until he could see out the ranch office window. Sam was riding Black Star and Jessica was sitting under the pecan tree watching him. Beside her lay Sheba, who was perkier than she'd been in a while. Jessica even tolerated that crazy monkey. At least with Jessica and her pennies around, Caesar wasn't bugging Matt so much.

As he watched, Jessica turned and looked back over her shoulder, then stood. From inside, Matt couldn't see down the road, but someone was obviously coming. Lita was already here, even though she'd discreetly avoided arriving in the early mornings—not that she'd find anything, since Matt always left Jessica's bed.

Just once he'd like to sleep all night in her arms, but

he'd promised himself he wasn't going to wish for what he couldn't have.

A ritzy black car pulled into the ranch yard. Not from around here, Matt noticed at once. No one around here could afford to drive fancy cars like that.

Jessica stood there, stone-faced. Briefly Matt wondered why she hadn't come inside to tell him they had a visitor, then the car door opened and an older dark-haired woman emerged.

She had on a jacket and pants the same color as the stones in his house, and right away Matt could see she was Jessica's type of classy.

He saw her give his place the once-over, then point to Sam in the paddock. Jessica cupped her hands to her mouth, then waved when she'd caught Sam's attention.

This, then, must be Sam's grandmother, the Fremont matriarch herself.

Jessica hadn't said much about her while she'd been here, and Matt elected to let them have their reunion in private.

Neither of the women was smiling.

Sam, bless him, remembered everything he'd been taught about dismounting, then climbed over the fence—he was an old hand at it now—and came running.

He flung himself at his grandmother in a way that made Matt's stomach feel hollow.

Well, he knew it had to end sometime. He just hadn't figured on it being today.

CHAPTER FOURTEEN

"GRAMMA, DID YOU SEE ME ride the horse?"

"Yes, I did."

Sam apparently didn't notice the tinge of disapproval in Rachel's voice, but Jessica did. She'd expected it, but she'd hoped that Rachel would spare Sam from her anger.

"I can even saddle him myself."

"Indeed."

"He rides very well, Rachel," Jessica said.

"And he's tired of it, is he?"

"Oh, no, Gramma! I love it here."

As Rachel gazed down at Sam, Jessica looked at him through her eyes. He was dusty and his new boots were filthy. His hair needed to be cut and his shirt was torn. She thought he looked like a little boy who was having a great summer, but she knew Rachel would think differently.

"You do appear to have been very casual here, Sam." Rachel looked around the ranch complex. The new shed stood out, making the other buildings look even shabbier than they usually did.

Caesar chose that inopportune moment to scurry up to Rachel.

She clutched her throat. "What's that!"

"Caesar's a monkey, Gramma. He knows tricks. Watch. Mom, do you have any money?"

"I don't have any more with me right now."

"That's okay." Sam twirled around and hopped from foot to foot, then held out his hand. "Coin."

To Jessica's surprise, Caesar took off. If she'd only known that nifty little trick a couple of weeks ago.

"Are you going to stay here, too, Gramma?"

What an excellent question, Jessica thought.

Rachel's face softened. "No, dear. I wanted to see you and speak with your mother."

"Here comes Caesar. Watch."

Chattering, Caesar came scurrying back, ran up to Sam and put a coin in his outstretched hand.

Sam put it in his mouth and bit it.

"Sam!" Jessica and Rachel said at the same time.

"It's part of the game," he told them, and put the coin into his pocket.

"Jessica," Rachel said, her voice strident. "Could we go inside?"

Here it comes, Jessica thought as she ushered Rachel toward the door. "Sam, you need to take care of Black Star."

"I *know,* Mom," he said, and ran off toward the paddock.

Lita, bless her heart, must have seen Rachel's arrival from the kitchen. A plate of gingersnaps was waiting on the coffee table in the den, and within moments of them sitting down, she appeared with tea in probably the only two cups of the heavy white china that were neither cracked nor chipped.

"Thank you, Lita," Jessica said. "Lita is our cook and housekeeper. This is Mrs. Fremont, Sam's grandmother."

For a moment, Jessica thought Lita was going to

curtsy. As it was, she bobbed her head and disappeared into the kitchen.

"I'm glad to see there are some civilizing aspects to this place," Rachel said.

Okay, so she wanted to take off the gloves. "I'm surprised to see you, since you never responded to my *daily* E-mails."

"You mean your little gloating messages? Certainly not."

Gloating? *Gloating?* Jessica was prevented from saying something she'd surely regret when Matt stepped into the den.

He looked so solid and strong and wonderful that Jessica just smiled at him for a moment.

It was undoubtedly the worst thing she could have done if she'd hoped to hide her feelings. When Rachel's breath hissed between her teeth, Jessica knew her mother-in-law had guessed why Jessica and Sam were still at Winter Ranch.

Well, so what? Jessica thought recklessly. "Rachel, this is Matt Winston. He owns the ranch." *And my heart.*

"Pleased to meet you, Mrs. Fremont."

"Mr. Winston," Rachel acknowledged icily.

Matt didn't let her intimidate him. "I see Lita has taken care of offering you refreshment. You're welcome to stay for supper if you like."

"Thank you, but I believe my business here will be concluded before then."

Matt's cordial expression didn't change. "Jessica, I'll go keep an eye on Sam." He strode toward the door and took his hat off the peg. "Ma'am," he said to Rachel. He caught Jessica's gaze just before he went out the door. She was learning to read his looks and that was one of encouragement.

She had a feeling she'd need it.

Rachel wasted no time with small talk. "Have—you—lost—your—mind?"

"No," Jessica answered, and dunked a gingersnap into her tea.

Rachel reached into her purse, put on her glasses and removed some folded papers. They were copies of bank transactions. Jessica's bank transactions, as it transpired.

"Fourteen thousand dollars as a donation to Lost Springs, I suppose I can live with, although the spectacle you made of yourself at the auction is still the hot topic of conversation. I can't enter a room without talk ceasing and people staring at me."

Once, Jessica would have cringed. Not anymore. "Oh, Rachel, it's probably because we've been so philanthropic lately. First you send those children to camp, then I buy a man at a bachelor auction. They're wondering whom we'll give money to next."

"Matthew Winston, apparently." Rachel shifted the papers. "You've bought building supplies, appliances, food...and what appears to be five thousand dollars in outright cash."

She made it all sound sordid. "How is it that you have access to my checking account?"

"It was your joint account with Samuel. His father and I always had signing privileges. After all, it's Fremont money," Rachel said pointedly.

"Which I've helped earn," Jessica replied, just as pointedly. Time for a chat with the bank and a new account. "I agreed to pay Matt for housing us here and teaching Sam about ranch life. In turn, he bought his building supplies from us." She smiled.

Rachel slowly removed her glasses and looked at her. "The man is broke, Jessica, and clearly stringing you along for all he can get, which is obviously quite a lot."

Ignore her. "He didn't ask. I offered."

"And I will not ask the particulars of what it was that you offered." Back on went the glasses. "I checked into him—"

"You had Matt *investigated?*"

"Of course! Did you think I wanted my only grandchild going off to some place I knew nothing about?"

"I'm here with him, Rachel." Jessica was finding it difficult to hold on to her temper.

"But your judgment is clearly flawed." Rachel read from the paper. "He came from Lost Springs, but we knew that. However, there is nothing of his life prior to that. He left Lost Springs and came here. Now, this ranch has an interesting history. It apparently passed from the Novak family—lost in a poker game, I believe?—to one Barnaby Schultz, a second-rate magician. Mr. Schultz bequeathed the ranch to Mr. Winston less than two years ago." Rachel looked at her. "The man is quite good-looking, I give you that, but, Jessica, he came from nothing and he has nothing."

Jessica gave her a direct look. "He has everything I want."

"Don't be vulgar."

"I wasn't. You are."

Removing her glasses, Rachel slipped them into their case and stuffed the papers back into her purse. "The man is a fortune hunter, Jessica. He is exactly the sort of man the Fremonts have always guarded against. But I don't blame you. You have been an exemplary daughter-in-law. These men always prey on our weaknesses and I'm aware that you are still young and attractive."

"Matt isn't like that."

"They're *all* like that." Rachel snapped her purse shut. "I've come to take Sam back with me."

"Sam doesn't want to leave yet. He likes it here. And he likes Matt. They get along great together."

Rachel winced as though in pain. "It isn't appropriate for him to remain here. Surely you realize that."

"Now just a minute—"

"And if you can't see that carrying on with a man in front of your son is wrong, then I must reevaluate your suitability as Sam's mother."

Jessica's jaw dropped. What was the matter with her? "I *am* Sam's mother. It's not a position you hold interviews for."

"I have only Sam's best interests at heart, as I'm sure you do. But others might question your judgment."

"What others?"

Rachel's eyes shifted before looking at Jessica defiantly. "There are laws that protect children in undesirable situations such as this."

Jessica barely recognized the woman who clutched her purse with white-knuckled hands. Or rather, she recognized her as the woman who'd years ago tried to keep her son from marrying Jessica. "Are you actually threatening to try to take Sam away from me?"

"Naturally I hope it won't come to that—"

"You're darn right it won't!" Jessica stood. "I'm going to get Sam so you can visit with him, but after that, feeling as you do, it would be best if you left."

"Not without my grandson."

"Rachel, you have no right to—"

She held up a hand. "Hear me out. Sam will come back with me. You may stay here until…until you have this man out of your system, and I will welcome you home. In the meantime, whatever decisions you make about your personal life, you will not be allowed to mortgage Sam's future."

"*What* are you talking about?"

"I have a court order denying you further access to all Fremont funds."

"I have never touched Fremont money! That money was money *I* earned! I've worked for the company for almost ten years." A court order? Rachel already had a court order? How easy would it be for her to get the same sympathetic judge to give her custody of Sam?

"*Fremont* Construction. The company is being held in trust for your son."

"I know that. I also know that if I hadn't found our niche market in providing custom work, there wouldn't be much of a company *to* be held in trust."

Rachel shook her head sadly. "That's why I know you'll thank me for keeping you from throwing it all away."

"I'm not throwing any of it away. I agreed to pay Matt for our room and board."

"Fine. Call it what you like, but there will be no more 'room and board' payments. Much as it pains me to see you disillusioned, I'd advise you to tell your lover that you have no more money to give him and then see how long he finds you irresistible."

So THAT WAS RACHEL FREMONT. Matt didn't like the woman much, but he figured there had to be some good in her if she was Sam's grandmother and Jessica had lived with her all these years. He understood that they'd had a disagreement, so he decided to spot her an insult or two.

But only to him, not Jessica or Sam.

He went looking for Sam and found him in the barn. "Hi, there. Looks like you did a good job putting up Black Star."

Sam gave him a quick look and went back to currying the horse. "My gramma's here."

"I saw her."

"We'll probably have to leave now."

Matt figured as much, too. Losing Jessica was bad enough, but he was going to miss working with Sam, miss having someone to talk to while he did chores. Miss seeing the boy grow up. He swallowed and kept his voice steady. "Well, we knew you'd have to go home sometime."

"Yeah, but I was going to try to get another week out of Mom."

Matt grinned, even though he'd already gone numb inside. He'd deal with the hurt later. Maybe they could come visit again. He almost said as much, but decided he'd better not.

Sam finished with Black Star. "Are Shelby and Tobias outside?"

Matt nodded.

Sam reached into his pocket. "Lita gave me cookies for them."

"You didn't tell her you fed them to the animals, did you?"

"She already knew. That's why she makes so many."

They couldn't go through the hole anymore, so they had to walk out front, then around the side of the barn. Sheba was sunning herself against the wall, looking a lot better. She might have a few years left in her after all, Matt thought. The vet had already told him he could halve the medicine he gave her in the injections, which, thanks to Jessica, he could afford. Maybe all the old tiger needed was a couple of good nights' sleep and some food. The hamburger seemed to do the trick.

As soon as the zebra and the mule saw Sam, they came trotting over to the fence. He stood on the bottom railing and handed them each a cookie.

Caesar chattered at them from the roof of the barn. Matt sighed. He was running out of coins for the fool monkey.

"I don't suppose your mom gave you any pennies?"

Sam shook his head. "You don't need them. Just dance for him."

"Dance for Caesar?"

"Yeah. You know, spin around and hop."

Matt didn't know. "And then what?"

Sam laughed. "Then you say 'coin.' Here, watch." Brushing off his hands, he hopped down from the fence. As Matt watched, he turned around in a circle, then hopped from one foot to the other a few times.

Caesar's head twitched as he followed Sam's movements. Sam added another spin, then shouted, "Coin!"

Caesar took off.

"Where's he going?" Matt asked.

Sam gave him a funny look. "To get a coin, of course."

Well, how about that? Sure enough, within a couple of minutes, Caesar scurried up to Sam.

Sam held out his hand and the monkey solemnly put a coin in it. Then Sam bit the coin.

Matt laughed and Sam did, too. "I think Caesar likes that part," Sam said. "Hey, look. This is another strange one." He handed it to Matt.

Matt stared. "It's gold. Where did it come from?"

"From Caesar."

"I meant before that. You say you've got others?"

Sam nodded.

When Barnaby needed money, he'd just spend a coin.

"So when you dance, Caesar brings you a coin?"

"Yeah. You want to try?"

Okay, for gold, Matt would dance for a monkey. In front of a giggling Sam, he turned around, then hopped from foot to foot.

Caesar squeaked.

"So what do you think? Worth a coin?"

Caesar took off, returning minutes later with another coin. It wasn't gold, but it was an Indian Head penny.

"Sam," Matt said, trying not to get too hopeful. "What do you say we try to find out where Caesar keeps his stash?"

"WHAT ARE THEY DOING?"

Jessica and Rachel looked out the front windows as Matt and Sam hopped and twirled their way across the ranch yard. Periodically Caesar would appear, then run away again.

"They're playing with the monkey," she replied just as Lita came into view and said something to Matt.

When Caesar next appeared, Sam got her to do the dance and Caesar took off. Jessica smiled.

Rachel's expression was pained. "The sooner my grandson is away from this place, the better."

Jessica faced her mother-in-law. "Sam likes it here. He's grown up a lot, Rachel. We've been babying him too much. Matt taught me that."

"*You* said he'd get tired of playing cowboy. Has he?"

Jessica shook her head. "Not yet."

"His life is back in Lightning Creek, Jessica."

"Is it? Or is it the life *we* want him to have?"

"He's too young to know what he wants. It's our responsibility to guide him." Rachel stood. "If you will not begin packing, then I will. Where is Sam's room?"

Jessica stayed by the front door. "If Sam doesn't want to leave, then I'm not going to make him."

Rachel's face was rigid. "You're being irresponsible. Any court will agree with me."

"Rachel, listen to yourself. That's twice you've threatened to drag the Fremont name through the courts in a nasty custody fight. Think of the nice, juicy story it will make for the newspapers." Jessica hadn't been a Fremont all this time for nothing.

Rachel changed tactics. "What about your job, then?"

"I've been doing it from here, haven't you noticed? The only thing I can't do is inspect sites and make bids. The new catalog is ready to go to press *and* I found an ironworker and wood carver."

At that moment, a familiar mufflerless rumble heralded the arrival of Frank's truck. Who would be driving it was anybody's guess.

Jessica looked outside, not at all surprised to see Frank emerge, turn around to help Carmen out and, finally, Katya. They spoke with Lita, who was gesturing animatedly toward the house. After a moment, they proceeded up the path.

"Some of Matt's friends are here to meet you." Jessica faced her mother-in-law. "Please remember that you are a Fremont and behave with all due civility."

Rachel's mouth dropped open at the same time the little group arrived at the door.

Carmen was in her best black, Katya was bedecked

with gold and Frank wore a suit and had slicked back his hair.

Jessica introduced everyone and stepped back as they sat down.

"So you are young Sam's grandmother," Carmen said, the leather sofa hissing under her weight. "He is a fine boy. So polite."

Frank nodded, his mustache quivering.

Katya added, "And my Krinkov says he's a smart one. He is very quick with the cards."

"Cards?" Rachel inquired with an ominous look at Jessica.

Carmen clutched both her throat and Katya's arm. "Katya, the muddiness of her aura...the mustard-yellow. Do you see it?" Carmen winced. "Such pain."

Making a tsking sound, Katya took Rachel's hand and studied it. "Oh, my dear," she said, covering her mouth and shaking her head. "Such a loss."

Rachel looked completely nonplussed.

"Which teacup is yours?" Carmen asked.

A bemused Rachel pointed, and Carmen had her swish the cup around before looking into it. "Yes, I see the loss...it has been in the past but affects you still. A husband?" she guessed.

"A child?" Katya asked.

Rachel's mouth quivered. "Yes!" she cried. "Yes!"

Katya patted her hand sympathetically. "Which?"

"My husband and my son."

Both women gasped, then moved closer to her, murmuring words of comfort. Rachel burst into tears.

"Old fish and crying women should best be left alone," Frank said, and gestured for Jessica to come with him outside.

She was relieved to escape.

"I believe I saw Matthew in the garage." Frank pointed. "Me, I am going to enjoy an afternoon nap under the tree."

Jessica heard chattering long before she saw Matt and Sam. The door to the garage was open and a folding ladder extended from the loft. Jessica climbed a couple of rungs and called, "Matt? Sam? Caesar?" The last was a whimsical addition.

"We're up here, Mom! We found Caesar's treasure and lots of other cool stuff."

Jessica climbed up the ladder and entered the world of The Amazing Molvano.

MATT COULD HARDLY BELIEVE that the best and worst days of his life were the same one. His relief at finding the source of the money Barnaby had used to keep the ranch going was tempered by the fact that Jessica would leave, if not within hours, then soon.

They had almost certainly made love for the last time.

According to Lita, that mother-in-law of Jessica's was throwing around some pretty heavy-handed threats. Matt was desperate to talk with her about it all, but not while Sam was here.

"There's an armoire in my room that looks like this stuff," Jessica said as she climbed up.

"It's all part of Barnaby's act." Matt reached out to help her up the last steps, letting his fingers linger on hers. "I used to love it when he showed me how his 'magic' worked. He didn't like to very often. Once he got the ranch, he decided he was a rancher, not a magician."

Stored in the garage attic were boxes and crates and huge props, all with The Amazing Molvano scrolled on them. When he'd been younger, before he'd decided to

be a rodeo champion, Matt had thought about bringing
The Amazing Molvano out of retirement.

"Matt, I'm ready to take the first load down," Sam
said.

"Yes, come see what we found, thanks to your son."
Matt led Jessica over to a divided trunk with holes at
the ends. "This is used for sawing assistants in half,"
he told her, then opened one end to reveal a huge pile
of money. "And by monkeys who want to hide coins."

"Will you look at that." Jessica stared at the monkey. "Caesar, you've been busy."

Caesar gave a mournful screech.

Matt and Sam had been filling silk scarves with the
coins so Sam could carry them down to the office for
sorting. "Barnaby would always talk about spending a
coin, and I never realized what he meant," Matt explained. "The circus people collected these over the
years and gave them to him to cover food and expenses
for the animals. I've had letters from coin dealers asking
if I had any more of the collection to sell, and I figured
it was all gone."

"Do you think he knew these were in here?"

Matt shook his head. "I don't know. He may have,
or maybe Caesar took them from where they originally
were. At any rate, I'm sure glad to have them back."
He tied two scarves together and draped the load around
Sam's neck. "Too heavy for you?"

"Nah," Sam said, and climbed down the ladder.

Matt peered over the edge until Sam made it all the
way down, then asked Jessica, "So how did it go with
Sam's grandmother?"

"Not good." Jessica related what her mother-in-law
had said, which was pretty much what Lita had told
him. He also knew Jessica was leaving out some things,

because occasionally she avoided his eyes by absently fingering the coins.

"So what's happening now?"

"I left her with Carmen and Katya."

Matt inhaled sharply. "I suppose that means she'll insist you two are out of here by dark."

Jessica sat on a black lacquer box and scooped coins into a scarf. "She told me that she'd take Sam back with her, but that I could stay here as long as I liked."

For one joyful moment, Matt thought he had it all, but he quickly returned to earth. He couldn't have anything if Jessica didn't have Sam. "So she *is* trying to take Sam away from you?"

"Not permanently." Jessica shrugged and tied the scarf into a knot. "What she's taking away is any Fremont money." She met his eyes. "Here we have a difference of opinion. She believes everything belongs to the Fremonts and I don't. I can dispute it, but until I do, I've been cut off. No more money."

"Because she doesn't want you and Sam to stay here?"

She nodded.

That was it then. Matt stared at the pile of coins. The money they'd bring from collectors was enough to keep the ranch going, but it wasn't enough for legal battles. And even if he'd been the richest man on earth, he wouldn't ask a woman to choose between him and her son.

He thought he'd numbed himself. He thought he was prepared for the pain.

He wasn't.

Matt turned away and searched through Barnaby's props for more handkerchiefs or scarves. She was being so casual and matter-of-fact. He was going to have to try to be the same. "So are you leaving before supper, or tomorrow morning?"

"What?"

"I wondered when you were leaving. Lita will want to know, too."

She stood. "Is that all you have to say?"

"What do you want me to say?"

"I want...I thought we..." Her composure threatened to break for the first time.

Matt hauled her into his arms. "I can't ask you to give up everything to stay here with me."

"You wouldn't be! Rachel's just making threats."

"Lita said she had legal papers."

Jessica sighed. "For the moment, yes—"

"Listen to me." Matt drew back so he could see her face. "A court took me from my mom. Yeah, it was the best thing, but it still hurt. You can't put Sam through that."

"Why do people keep telling me how to raise my son!" Jessica pushed away from him. "Why do they keep telling me how to live my life? What's wrong with the way I want to live it?"

Matt shook his head.

"I don't want to go back. I don't want to live like the perfect Fremont anymore and I don't want Sam living that way, either."

She couldn't see what would happen, but Matt could. "You've never been poor in your life, have you?"

"Oh, please. Don't tell me you're a reverse snob."

"I'm realistic. You wouldn't last very long without money. You'd hate being broke and you'd come to hate me."

"Give me *some* credit, Matt."

"Funny you should use those words."

She stared at him. "Unless you don't *want* me to stay. Is that it?"

Of course he wanted her to stay. "Not like this."

Jessica looked as though he'd slapped her. "Are we arguing about money again?"

She couldn't fight for Sam without it. "I guess so."

Jessica rubbed her forehead. "Say by a whole lot of bad luck, Rachel convinces some judge that I don't have any right to the money I've earned. Shouldn't doing without it be my decision?"

"Not entirely, no."

An awful silence followed. Jessica wrapped her arms around herself. "I see."

Matt didn't think she did. "It's been great having you here. This last week has meant—"

"Stop." She closed her eyes tightly. "I can write the rest of the script myself."

JESSICA BLINDLY STUMBLED out of the attic and down the stairs. Rachel was right. It was all about money.

Hadn't Jessica meant anything to him?

Oh, she supposed if she'd let him finish his kiss-off speech, he would have tried to let her down gently.

She didn't want gentle. She wanted a great big painful crash landing so she'd remember it the next time she was tempted back into the wonderful world of relationships. Never again. This was it. She didn't need them.

Jessica stormed into the ranch house, ready to pack and leave.

"Jessica?" Rachel called. "What's wrong?"

Jessica stopped long enough to take in the three women on the leather sofa and the fact that they apparently were on very good terms. Swell. "What's wrong is that you were right, Rachel. He was only interested in me for my money. Happy now? I'm packing."

"Who? Who is this who is interested in your money?" Katya demanded.

"Matt."

"No." She shook her head, earrings bobbing.

Carmen heaved herself off the sofa and went to the door. "Frank, wake up!" She clapped her hands. "Go get Matthew right now. Bring him here." She turned back around and pointed to a chair. "You. Sit."

Jessica sat, but only because she didn't think she could go one-on-one with Carmen and win.

"Your Matthew seems very nice," Rachel said.

Jessica stared at her.

"Carmen and Katya have been telling me all about him."

Had they put something in her tea?

And could she have some?

A few minutes later, Matthew arrived. Carmen immediately pointed to a chair opposite Jessica. "Sit."

He, too, sat.

"Now, what's all this about you only liking this girl for her money?"

"I never said that."

Jessica couldn't let that pass. "You dropped me as soon as you found out I didn't have any money!"

Matt's jaw set, but he didn't deny it.

"There can be no dropping," Katya said. "You two have ridden the elephant together. You are betrothed."

"What?" cried three voices.

Carmen nodded. "She rode the elephant with him," she said to Rachel. "He asked and she said yes. They were alone together."

"We were on an elephant!" Jessica pointed out.

"Did I not say just that?"

"It was not unexpected," Carmen added. "She redid the kitchen."

"Yes. All new," Katya said.

"Jessica?" Rachel raised her eyebrows, but she didn't look angry. In fact, her face seemed softer than it had been for years.

"He needed…" She gave up. "Yes. I fixed up the kitchen."

Katya made a "so there" gesture. "Now, what is the trouble between you two?"

Matt stared straight ahead. "I will never separate a woman from her child."

Carmen looked stern. "Has anyone asked you to?"

Matt jerked his head toward Rachel. "Mrs. Fremont threatened Jessica."

Everyone's eyes turned toward Rachel.

"I—I plan to take Sam home. I told Jessica she could stay."

Carmen and Katya looked at each other. "And this is a problem?" Katya asked.

"She has them papers in her purse." Lita pointed from the kitchen doorway.

Rachel looked defiant once more. "I may have been mistaken about Matthew—*may*—but I will protect Sam's inheritance."

At their puzzled expressions, Jessica explained. "The Fremont money is held in trust for Sam. Rachel is afraid I'll spend too much of it here."

Carmen wagged her finger. "You spend a lot."

"It was mine!"

"Shh!" Katya held out her hands. "You have no money?"

"Apparently not." Jessica threw a defiant look toward Rachel.

"What about you?" Katya asked her. "You got money?"

"I...it's my grandson's money."

Muttering in her native tongue, Katya removed one of her gold bracelets and picked up Rachel's hand. Before anyone could say anything, she'd worked the bracelet onto Rachel's wrist. Then she came across the room and did the same for Jessica. "Now you two got money."

Feeling her face grow hot, Jessica stared down at the thin bangle gleaming against her wrist, then up at Matt.

"I'm a woman of means again," she said.

"Jessica," he whispered, his face both sad and tender.

In the background, Rachel started to sob. "I'm not a horrible person, I'm not!"

"'Course you're not," Carmen said. "Your son's wife stayed with you all that time, didn't she?"

"But Sam's all I have left!"

Matt caught Jessica's eye and gestured to Rachel. "You see? I can't make you choose between me and your son."

"Nobody's going to be choosing between nobody," Katya said. "We're gonna work it all out. There's gonna be lots of visiting. Young Sam will visit his grandmother and give the newlyweds some privacy, and Rachel will come here as often as she likes."

"Build her a house," Carmen said.

Katya shrugged. "She can build her own house. She's got that company. Anyway," she went on, "Rachel is gonna have a house here and can see her grandson all the time if she wants. And when she's not visiting him, she'll be playing bridge with us. I love my Krinkov, but he is not a good fourth. He cheats.''

Just then, Sam came into the room carrying a coin-filled scarf. ''Look at these. I sorted the neatest ones in here.'' He knelt at the coffee table and opened the scarf.

''Ah.'' Carmen picked up one of the coins. ''This one was from the old country…''

Over a still-crying Rachel, Katya motioned for them to leave. ''You go. We will talk.''

Matt and Jessica slipped outside and headed toward the pecan tree where Frank had been napping. The breeze picked up and something fell from the tree, landing with a metallic thunk on Rachel's car.

''My wallet!'' Jessica laughed and picked it up. Other than a few monkey bites, it looked in surprisingly good condition.

''I guess this means you can leave anytime you want to.''

She heard the uncertainty in his voice. Looking him squarely in the eyes, she said, ''I don't want to leave. I don't want Sam to leave, either.''

Matt took a deep breath. ''If you stay, I want it to be for good.''

''Well, I wouldn't want it to be for bad. And even though Katya and the others seem to be bringing Rachel around, there's going to be quite an adjustment. There's also my job and Sam changing schools and…'' She stopped, suddenly uncertain. ''But I may be presuming too much based on just one elephant ride.''

He grinned and took her in his arms. ''I love you and I intend to hold you to the elephant betrothal.''

Jessica felt her heart warm. ''I love you, too, and the elephant ride works for me.''

''I think we've just worked out the most important

detail. The rest will fall into place.'' Matt smiled down at her. ''You realize that everyone is watching us, don't you?''

''I would expect them to.''

His eyes darkened. ''And you also realize that I'm going to kiss you now, don't you?''

Jessica drew her arms around his neck. ''Better make it a good one, then.''

And he did.

continues with

SHANE'S LAST STAND

by

Ruth Jean Dale

Dinah Hoyt was chosen by the good citizens of
Bushwack, Colorado, to "buy" former Bushwack
resident Shane Daniels at auction...and then talk him
into using his celebrity to save Old Pioneer Days.
Everyone knew that she and Shane had once been
close. But no one knew exactly *how* close, or what
had come of that teenage love affair...not even Shane.
And if Dinah had anything to say about it, he wasn't
going to find out!

Available in February

Here's a preview!

CHAPTER SIX

DINAH HAD NEVER DANCED with Shane before.

Incredible as that seemed, the truth was that they'd never gone out in public as a couple, never publicly acknowledged the irresistible attraction between them. With the exception of gossip at Bushwack High School, nothing had linked them romantically in the public mind.

In his arms beneath swirling lights at the Thirsty Buzzard, she felt a sense of disbelief, almost as if this were happening in a dream instead of in a honky-tonk in Tall Timber, Colorado.

Despite the sore ribs, there was no hesitancy in Shane's movements. He was a professional athlete and she'd expected him to be a good dancer, which he was. He held her at just the proper distance with just the proper firmness, leading her smoothly through a good old Texas two-step.

She found herself smiling, really getting into the dance and the occasion. Her life had been a series of catastrophes for years and there'd been few opportunities to really let her hair down and just have fun.

And this *was* fun. Her hand and her waist tingled beneath his light hold, and she grew even more breathless than she could attribute to just the exertion of the dance.

"Ladies' choice!" the leader of the band spoke into

the microphone, never missing a beat on the guitar draped across his front. Almost before she realized what was happening, Dinah felt a light tap on her shoulder. Looking around, she saw a smiling woman standing there.

The smile was for Shane, of course. The newcomer said, "Excuse me!" and stepped in front of Dinah. With a shrug, Shane took the woman in his arms and whirled her away.

Annoyed, Dinah turned to walk off the dance floor. A cowboy standing nearby gave her a crooked smile. "Sorry my date made off with your fella. Bull riders!" He rolled his eyes. "They're the rock stars of rodeo, I reckon, always havin' to fight the women off with a stick. I should be so lucky."

Dinah had to laugh at that. Bull riders *were* the glamour boys, probably because what they did was so incredibly dangerous that just being in their presence was a thrill for many.

Not her, of course.

Over the cowboy's shoulder she saw Shane holding the short curvy brunette. Dinah looked quickly away as an almost perverse pleasure washed over her.

Half the women in this saloon might be looking for a chance to dance with Shane but he was going home with her. Even though there was nothing between them now and hadn't been for a very long time, she didn't have to stand in line for his attention.

Eat your heart out, girls.

Harlequin Historicals®
Historical Romantic Adventure!

From rugged lawmen and valiant knights to defiant heiresses and spirited frontierswomen, Harlequin Historicals will capture your imagination with their dramatic scope, passion and adventure.

Harlequin Historicals . . . they're too good to miss!

HARLEQUIN®
Presents

The world's bestselling romance series...
The series that brings you your favorite authors,
month after month:

Helen Bianchin...Emma Darcy
Lynne Graham...Penny Jordan
Miranda Lee...Sandra Marton
Anne Mather...Carole Mortimer
Susan Napier...Michelle Reid

and many more uniquely talented authors!

Wealthy, powerful, gorgeous men...
Women who have feelings just like your own...
The stories you love, set in exotic, glamorous locations...

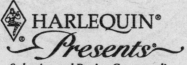

HARLEQUIN®
Presents

Seduction and Passion Guaranteed!

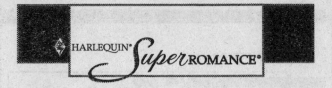
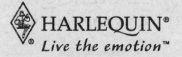

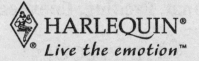

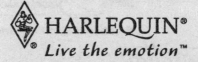

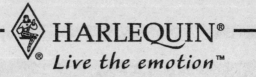

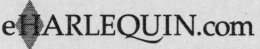